DEATH OF A WALLABY

The Wobbly Wallaby II

MIKE SKILLICORN

Published by Skill Creative in 2018
Cover Design by Nieves Barreto
Instagram: @nievesbarretoart

ISBN-13: 978-0-9945088-3-6

www.thewobblywallaby.com

For Gus.

CONTENTS

REUNITED

"Jake! Peg! Over here!" shouted Wally, trying to catch their attention.

He watched Jake stop sharply, his ears twitching, trying to locate the source of the call. Peg had to sidestep abruptly to avoid running into him.

"Over here!"

Jake looked up and spotted Wally. A wide grin spread across his face. Peg followed Jake's gaze and found him too, standing at the top of the ridge.

"Wally!" she exclaimed, and the three wallabies hopped towards each other just as the rain began to fall more heavily.

"You made it!" Jake shouted as he approached. "I can't believe it!" He bounded in and wrestled Wally to the ground in a friendly tussle.

"Steady, mate! I'm a bit knocked around," said Wally, still aching from his impact with the ledge. "Glad to see you made it too!" he said, overjoyed that the three were back together again.

As Wally got to his feet, Peg greeted him with a big, welcoming hug. In an instant, Darcy was out of Peg's pouch, across her shoulder, and onto Wally's head.

"Woohoo!" he cried, dancing between Wally's ears. "We made it! We made it!"

"Thank heavens you're okay, Wally! You had me so worried!" said Peg. "We couldn't see you once we'd climbed the wall. Not on this side or the other. I thought those dingoes had finally caught you. How on earth did you get up here?"

"Across the Leap," Wally replied, still reeling from the encounter with Knuth. "But it was close. The dingoes cut me off and forced me up the ramp. Once I was up there, I knew there was nowhere else to go. The Leap was my only option. I was terrified, trying to decide which was worse: getting torn apart by those dingoes or falling onto the rocks at the bottom of the Leap. To be honest, I didn't think I had that jump in me.

"It wasn't exactly a smooth landing though," he continued. "My legs twisted up underneath me when I landed, and I smashed into the cliff at the back of the ledge. That knocked the wind right out of me. Then I looked back and saw the leader of the pack, the one with the big fang, jump after me. He almost made it too. His claws dug into the ledge and he tried to drag himself up." Wally shuddered, the horrible vision of the big dingo flashing through his mind.

"But he must have lost his footing at the last moment, because suddenly he slipped and fell back into the chasm. He scared the life out of me, that dingo. I could barely move, and he was dragging himself up right in front of me." A shiver ran up Wally's back as he remembered Knuth's face, so determined, so intent.

"He had some nerve, I'll say that for him," Wally continued. "It was a big jump for me but an incredible jump for a dingo. He must have been strong."

"Strong and ferocious!" Peg added. "I was petrified in the clearing!"

"So was I," Wally admitted. "But what else could we have done? I'm just glad it all worked out. How did you go getting up the wall?"

"We were up that wall so fast, I can't even remember climbing it!" Jake laughed. "We had some trouble from those two eagles, but our early warning system saved the day," he said, nodding at Darcy.

Darcy raised his arms in his best muscle-man pose.

"You made it pretty easy for us, Wally," said Peg. "All the dingoes went after you. By the time we got to the top of the wall, you and the dingoes were gone. We thought you might have tried to lure them out into the open again. Then we heard the howls, and we thought they were howling because they'd finally caught you. We've been trying to find a lookout, but no matter where we went, we couldn't see you."

"It took me a while to get back on my feet," Wally said. "I hit the ledge pretty hard. I've got a few bruises, but I'm sure I'll be okay." He paused, then noticed the cut on Peg's shoulder. "Looks like I'm not the only one who had a close call."

"Oh, that's nothing!" said Peg. "Just a little souvenir from one of those eagles." She smiled. "But what about the rest of the dingoes? What happened to them?"

"We don't have to worry about the dingoes anymore," said Wally, visibly relieved. "I watched them from the ledge for a while, but none of them dared try the Leap after what happened to their leader. They stood and howled for a while at the top of the ramp, but eventually they just turned and left. It was such a relief to watch them walk away."

"Good riddance to all of them, especially the leader. I still can't believe you walked straight up to him in the clearing," Jake said. "Fancy telling a dingo to get out of your way! I thought we were goners for sure!"

The wallabies burst into laughter, though it had been anything but funny at the time.

"So did I!" said Peg. "That was the craziest plan ever. You are completely mad, Wally," she added, giving him a playful shove. "Completely!"

"Well, we're all still here, aren't we?" he protested, smiling, fully aware how close they had come to a less favourable outcome. "And can you believe it? It's raining!"

"I know, but who cares about that!" Peg said. "Look at this place! It's so green! It's paradise!"

"And I'm hungry!" said Jake.

The rain fell more heavily then, but none of them cared. They danced in the cool, refreshing downpour. It was just so good to feel the rain again, and there was so much to eat!

They all ate until their bellies were fit to burst. Then Jake raised the question they'd been asking since the adventure began.

"So, where to now?"

Wally looked around at the fertile land. "It's a bit hard to say," he said, unable to hide his grin. "There are so many options."

He gazed out at the river that cut the valley in two and to the expansive fields that lay on either side. He remembered the last time the wallabies had stood together on a ridge, looking for direction. They had truly come a long way.

"Why don't we head to that river," suggested Peg. "That big river. With the cool running water." She started to smile again.

Wally looked over at Jake, who remembered too.

"Refreshing and clean, like it's just fallen from the sky," they all said in unison, and burst out laughing again.

"The river it is then," said Wally. "Hang on, Darcy, we're going for a hop."

CAPER'S RUN

The three dingoes made their way slowly down the ramp, dragging their mood along with their feet. When they finally reached the base, it was Caper who spoke.

"I'm going to go and look for Knuth."

"Why?" asked Ringo. "He's dead. Nothing could survive that fall. Not even him."

Caper was surprised by the response. "I know he's dead, but he was our leader. He deserves some respect."

"He was a cold-hearted mongrel, is what he was," argued Bomber. "Scared the life out of me with that tooth of his. He's got all the respect he's ever going to get from me."

"You were happy enough to follow him when he was alive," Caper said, the loathing clear in his voice. "Besides," he added, "have you got somewhere else to be? We've spent weeks tracking those wallabies and now we're going back empty-handed." The words stuck in his throat as his frustration began to rise. "And now one of us is dead and you can't even spend five minutes with him?"

"He led us out here!" snapped Bomber. "And it's an awfully long way back."

"You didn't have to come," Caper said, though he knew that wasn't quite true. Any kind of insubordination in the pack would have sent Knuth into a furious rage. Not that he could ever remember seeing that happen, he'd never known anyone to stand up to Knuth. No one, except for that wretched wallaby.

"Anyway, there's no reason to rush back, is there?" Caper continued. "What difference is it going to make if we spend a couple of minutes looking for him?" He paused to let that sink in, waiting for a reaction. Neither moved.

"You're wasting your time," insisted Bomber. "And I'm not going to waste mine looking for a dead dingo. You go for your life, Caper. I'm staying here."

"What about you, Ringo?"

"I'm with Bomber. We'll give you ten minutes, then we're heading back. The last waterhole is a long way away, it's already stinking hot, and the day isn't getting any cooler."

Caper grunted in disgust at the two dingoes, then turned and made his way through the bush to find Knuth. He was in a foul mood now. Not only had the pack lost its leader, but he'd also lost Knuth's protection, and it had all been for nothing.

They had failed to catch any of the wallabies, and now he was stuck with two dingoes he didn't like, and he was sure the feeling was mutual.

Caper walked to the clearing, not caring at all if the other two were there when he returned. He knew the pack would break apart now. The other two would never let a smaller dingo lead, and there was no way he was going to follow their orders. After all, he reasoned, he had more brains than the pair of them put together.

When he reached the end of the clearing, Caper turned and entered the gap between the cliff wall and the ramp, the shadows casting a gloom over the rocks that seemed to match his sullen mood.

Knuth wasn't hard to find. Among the fallen trees and rocks, his big, broken body lay motionless on the ground. Caper approached slowly, still feeling small in the presence of the fearless dingo.

"You crazy dog," he muttered. "Why did you have to go and jump?"

He sniffed at Knuth and sat for a moment, the stillness of the great dog unnerving him. A part of him willed Knuth to wake up, to rise from the rocks so things could go back to the way they were, but he knew that was foolishness. Knuth was gone, and things would never be the same again.

He lowered his head as he thought of Knuth

and the wallabies, letting his wrath stew. The more he thought about it, the worse it got.

When he finally raised his head again to look at Knuth, a fierce determination filled his eyes. "You wouldn't give up, would you?"

Vengeance had found its way into Caper in the dark shadows of the gap and had already begun to consume him. There was a score to settle now. He would find those wallabies if it was the last thing he ever did.

But how would he get over the wall? He couldn't stop thinking about the Leap. If Knuth couldn't make it, he had no chance. Knuth was strong and powerful, and Caper knew he didn't share that strength. He would be lucky to jump half as far.

"There must be a way," he thought, as he got up and made his way back through the gap, deciding to take one more look at the boulders that the other two wallabies had climbed. But as he walked down the length of another fallen tree, a dangerous idea sparked in his mind.

He paused, struck momentarily by genius, until the idea became a plan.

With a surge of renewed enthusiasm, he raced back to Bomber and Ringo.

He found them lying listlessly in the dirt.

"Come on, you two, we're going back up the ramp."

"What for?" asked Ringo. "You're not going to jump."

"I think I might know how to get across," Caper replied.

"You'll never make that jump," said Bomber. "Look at you, you skinny little thing. You'd be lucky to clear your own shadow."

Ringo chuckled.

Caper stopped and looked Bomber squarely in the eye. "Those wallabies have beaten us every time. Beaten you. If you can live with that, then you're even less of a dingo than I thought. I may have a way to get to the other side of that wall. If you want to catch those wallabies, come with me. Otherwise, turn tail and head back to that lifeless ridge like a coward."

Caper turned and began walking briskly up the ramp, desperately hoping the two would follow. He was going to need their help.

"He's crazy," said Ringo, surprised by Caper's sudden determination. "He'll never get across that gap."

"I know," Bomber replied flatly, stung by Caper's words. "I don't know what on earth he's thinking, but I'm going up to find out."

"Come on, Bomber. It's a long way up that ramp. Do you really want to chase that little runt up there again?"

"I'm not going up there for nothing. I'm sick of

that little pup. It's about time he was put in his place. If he doesn't have a good reason for me to be up there, one less dingo will be coming back down."

A sinister chuckle rattled in Ringo's throat as the two dingoes got to their feet and followed Caper up the ramp.

Caper arrived at the Leap well before Bomber and Ringo and immediately found what he was looking for. A fallen tree lay a short distance from the end of the ramp. He walked over, bit down on a branch, and tried to drag it towards the edge. The tree refused to budge. He braced himself and tried again, straining against the weight, but it was no use. The tree wouldn't move.

Bomber laughed at the sight of the small dingo as he and Ringo appeared at the top of the ramp.

"What are you trying to do with that?"

"I'm moving it over to the Leap," replied Caper confidently.

"You'll never move that, you little runt."

"I'd like to see you do any better," Caper spat, furious at being called a 'runt'. He hated the word and it had dogged him since birth. The last and smallest of his litter, he'd always had to rely on his wits to survive. Part of that meant never showing any fear. "You talk big, Bomber, but it's all hot air to me."

"Get out of the way, you skinny little thing," said Bomber, taking up the challenge. "Come on, Ringo, lend a hand."

Locking their jaws on a branch each, the three dingoes strained against the weight of the log and gradually it started to move. Slowly at first, but every tiny shift added to Caper's determination.

"Heave!" he cried.

It wasn't easy work in the heat, but soon they had managed to manoeuvre the trunk so that a little more than half of the thin end extended beyond the Leap toward the ledge on the other side.

The tree teetered on the edge, but Caper quickly threw his weight across it to bring it back down. He stood up on the trunk, looking down the narrow pole that he was going to run along. If he could just get to the end, it was a much shorter jump across, as long as the thick end of the tree didn't start to lift while he was suspended over the gap.

Then he looked down at the fall he would take if he missed the jump or lost his footing while he ran across. His stomach dropped at the thought.

"So what now, genius?" asked Bomber. "It's not long enough."

"You two lie across the base of the trunk. I'm going to run out and jump."

"You're kidding, aren't you? You're going to

jump?" Bomber couldn't believe his ears.

"Oh, I've got to see this," said Ringo, laughing.

"So we just lie across here, right?" he said, as he put his weight across the base of the trunk. "I hope you brought your wings with you!"

"This is going to be funny," muttered Bomber as he joined Ringo at the base of the tree.

The taunts only fuelled Caper's resolve. Falling would be a better fate than having to put up with Bomber and Ringo any longer. He walked slowly back around behind the two dingoes.

"Okay, we're ready, super dog! Let's see you fly!"

Caper paused behind the trunk, looking down its length one last time. He had chosen well, the tree was remarkably straight and even. He took one final look at the ledge on the other side and took off, before the thought of what he was about to do could change his mind.

He leapt over Bomber and Ringo, landing nimbly on the log, and sprinted out over the Leap. As he approached the end of the tree, he pushed off with all his might.

He sailed through the air, the terror of falling twisting him up inside as he flew across the abyss, but the fear was short-lived. He landed gracefully on the ledge on the other side.

"What the?" exclaimed Bomber, stunned. "How did he do that?"

Not wanting to be outdone by the smaller dingo, Bomber jumped to his feet and quickly made his way back to where Caper had started his run.

"Stay there, Ringo," he commanded. "If that little runt can do it, so can I."

"Wait, Bomber!" shouted Ringo. "You're too heavy!"

But there was no stopping him. Bomber leapt over Ringo and started to race out along the trunk, his weight lifting the base off the ground.

"No, no, nooooo!" howled Ringo, as he rose higher and higher into the air.

Ringo had been right, Bomber's weight had tipped the trunk well before he was anywhere near the end of the run. Bomber yelped as he realised what was happening and stopped abruptly, sealing the fate of the two dingoes.

The tree jack-knifed up until a thick branch caught on the edge of the ramp, locking the two dingoes into a deadly, one-way seesaw. Bomber wrapped himself around the log and any branch within reach, his claws scratching for something to hold onto. Slowly, he descended further into the chasm as his end of the log swung back towards the Leap.

As Bomber's end fell, Ringo's end rose with increasing speed. The log slammed into the side of the ramp, sending Ringo flying out over the chasm and into a horrifying free-fall, accompanied by his unearthly howl.

The force of the impact snapped the branch that was caught on the edge, sending the tip of the tree spearing into a clump of rocks directly under the edge of the Leap.

With Bomber's weight now over the gap, the thick end of the tree swung in a slow and graceful arc across the Leap. Bomber yelped as he watched the inevitable unfold. The trunk crashed onto the ledge on the far side with a juddering bang, finally breaking his grip on the log. With a pitiful cry, he began his long descent to the bottom of the Leap.

The tree bounced and shuddered before finally finding its resting place, miraculously bridging the gap between the two sides.

"I'll be blowed," thought Caper, staring at the tree in amazement. "How did those two fools manage that?"

He stepped cautiously over to the edge and looked down. There, in the shadows at the bottom of the chasm, lay the three lifeless dingoes.

"Looks like those two got to see Knuth one last time after all," he thought to himself, realising he was now all that remained of the pack.

Alone, he turned and made his way up the dusty track to the lookout, following in Wally's fresh footsteps.

THE CROSSING

The wallabies moved quickly through the bush, elated but alert. Everything was new again, and until they became familiar with their new territory, they couldn't afford to let their guard down. The last thing they wanted was to swap one pack of dingoes for another.

It was almost dusk when they reached the edge of the bush-covered hills that led to the river; all that separated them now was a flat, grassy plain.

"It seems so close!" said Peg, barely able to control her urge to keep going.

"I know," said Wally, "but it doesn't make sense to race down there tonight. It's getting dark and we've got good cover here. The river will still be there in the morning."

Peg and Jake knew he was right. No one had forgotten the events at Roughneck's Puddle, so it didn't take much to convince them of the possible danger. Reluctantly, the wallabies stayed at the edge of the bush, settling down on a soft patch of grass overlooking the plain.

"How long do you think it's been since we drank from a proper river?" Peg asked.

Wally thought back to the land where the three of them had grown up. "Longer than I can remember." He struggled to recall drinking from a single river in his life. He'd seen a stream or two, but they were nothing like the size of the river on the other side of the plain.

"My dad used to talk about a river," said Jake. "But it didn't make much sense to me. I've never seen anything like the river he described. Then again, not much of what he said ever made sense to me. He died years ago. Maybe it's just not as wet as it used to be."

Wally thought of the commander of their mob and his refusal to move the mob on. "Hard to know," was all he offered.

"Well, I can't wait to get there. And it's just one more sleep away," Peg chirped, lying down on the soft grass.

Darcy, having slept through most of the journey through the bush, finally pushed his tiny head out of Peg's pouch.

"Just look at this place!" he said. "So many green trees to choose from! Just think of all that sap! I might just pop out and have a look around, if that's okay with everyone."

"All right, but be careful," said Peg, surprising

herself with the warning. She had grown quite fond of the little sugar glider. She lifted Darcy out of her pouch and carried him over to a gum tree that stretched into the heavens, setting him gently on a branch.

"Don't go too far. We don't want to lose you."

"No worries," he said over his shoulder. As quick as a flash, Darcy was up the side of the tree.

"Stay out of trouble," Peg said softly, knowing Darcy couldn't hear her. She watched him disappear into the leaves of the tree, then shook her head and returned to Wally and Jake. Jake was already asleep.

She settled back into the soft grass, so different from the stony dirt they used to call a bed. She rested her head gently above her paws, and within minutes her eyes had closed and thoughts of the river filled her dreams.

* * *

Darcy didn't have to go far to find what he was looking for. The trees were thick with sugary sap and crawling with juicy insects. For the first time in a long time, food was plentiful, and Darcy made the most of it, tasting every morsel.

He went from tree to tree, feasting on the delicious bushland smorgasbord, eating until his belly ached. When he had finally eaten more than his fill, he started to make his way back. "I'm too heavy to glide!" he thought as he ambled along a branch that sheltered the wallabies. He'd eaten so much it felt like his belly was dragging against the branches as he walked. He began to climb back down the tree when he spied a tiny hollow in the trunk that looked cosy and dry. Without a second thought, he crawled inside and snuggled up.

"As it should be," he thought, as his eyes finally closed for the night.

* * *

The dawn was long gone by the time Wally woke, having overslept on the comfort of the soft grass. He jumped up quickly, realising he'd slept in, then saw that he wasn't the only one who had enjoyed the luxury of the thick grass. Jake and Peg were still fast asleep.

He stood and stretched, scratching his ears with his paws and quickly scanned the area. He considered letting them sleep, but he couldn't resist the call of the river. He woke Peg easily, then went to work rousing Jake.

"Is Darcy back?" asked Peg.

"I haven't seen him. I'm sure he'll be around somewhere."

Peg looked up into the tree she had set him on the night before.

"Darcy!" she called, but there was no answer.

"Darcy!" she called again, her eyes scanning the branches for movement.

Once Wally had finally managed to wake Jake, the two wandered over to help Peg.

"Didn't the little bloke come back last night?" Jake asked, looking up into the tree.

"No," said Peg, now starting to worry. "I hope he's all right. This place is so new, who knows what comes out around here after dark."

"I'm sure he's fine. Just look for a tree with a hollow," said Jake casually. "Look, there's one right there." He hopped over and thumped on the trunk with his foot.

"Hey Darcy! Are you up there?"

The thumping woke Darcy with a fright. He was cranky when he poked his little head out of the hollow.

"Jeez, Jake! Can't you let a bloke sleep? I've been up all night! Oh, my stomach... I'm still so full."

"Come on, Darcy, you'll have to come down," called Wally. "We're going to the river."

"Okay, okay!" Darcy rubbed the sleep from his eyes and made his way slowly down the trunk, grumbling under his breath. Peg lifted him off the branch and settled him back into her pouch, where he yawned and went straight back to sleep.

"He's tired."

"I can't blame him if he's been up all night," said Wally. "We went through an awful lot yesterday, we should all be exhausted. I have to say though, that was the best sleep I've had in ages."

"I know," said Jake, "I could've slept all day."

"You'd sleep all day every day if you had the chance," teased Peg.

"Come on, you two. Let's just get down to that river. I'm getting thirsty just thinking about it."

They crossed the flat land that led to the river in no time and were soon standing at the top of the bank, looking down at the clear water sweeping around a bend and flowing quickly past them.

"Look at all that water!" exclaimed Peg, having never seen a river so wide or so deep. "How can there possibly be so much water here and so little back home?" It seemed terribly unfair that something could be so plentiful in one place, but so desperately scarce in another. "There's enough here for a thousand wallabies!"

"At least a thousand," Wally replied. The river was much wider than it had appeared from the lookout at the Divide, and the rich, fertile smell of it now filled the air.

"Okay, who's going in first this time?" asked Jake. "I'm running a bit short of tail." The memory of his last swim was still fresh in his mind.

"I doubt there'd be crocodiles in there. The water's moving too quickly, don't you think?" Peg replied, sensing Jake's concern.

"I hope you're right. There's no sign of any tracks on the bank either," said Jake. "Come on, this is too good to watch. I'm going down for a drink. Who's with me?"

"I'm in front of you!" Peg joked, hopping past Jake to be the first at the water's edge.

The water was fresh and clear, and tasted delicious. They splashed in the shallows, being careful not to be drawn into the current, playing in the cool, clear water. It was a far cry from the muddy puddles they used to call waterholes.

After a while, Jake, now more confident in the river and less worried about crocodiles, started drifting into deeper waters. Sensing the danger, Wally slid quietly alongside Peg and whispered, "Watch this."

"Jake!" he shouted, acting horrified. "There's something behind you!"

Jake was out of the water so fast, he was dry before he reached the bank.

Wally and Peg collapsed in the shallows, roaring with laughter as Jake turned around and realised he'd been tricked.

"That's not even funny!" he howled. "Not even partly funny! Wait until you get half your tail bitten off. We'll see how much you like it!"

That just made Wally and Peg laugh louder.

"Okay, maybe it was a bit funny," admitted Jake. "But don't do that again! You scared another four inches off my tail!"

"You should've seen the look on your face, Jake!" Peg said between fits of laughter.

Slowly, Jake came around, and soon he was laughing too, though more out of relief than anything else.

Wally and Peg climbed out of the water to the sound of Jake's good-natured grumbling, and the three of them chewed their way through a good breakfast. With their bellies full, they lazed in the warmth of the morning sun.

"I'm so full," Jake moaned as he lay on the bank. "If I eat one more blade of grass, I'm going to explode."

"Me too," said Wally.

"You two had better watch it, or you'll end up looking like a pair of wombats," Peg teased. "You don't have to binge anymore. It would take forever to eat all this food. And the river, it's all just incredible."

"It sure is," said Jake. "It's like a wallaby paradise."

"Mmm," Wally murmured contentedly. He couldn't have imagined a place so green and plentiful, especially having grown up in the dry landscape he once called home. "Paradise."

He rolled over so the sun could bake his other

side, letting his thoughts wander as he gazed over the water and the thick grass lining the banks. Peg was right; there was enough food and water here for a lifetime. They would never have to worry about starving again. It seemed a worthy reward for all they had been through, and here he was, with his two best friends, finally free of the dingoes and enjoying the bounty. Life couldn't get much better.

"Hey, look!" cried Peg, jarring Wally from his thoughts. "There's a couple of wallabies like us on the other side of the river!"

"Where?" asked Wally, scanning the opposite bank.

"There. Next to that big gum tree."

Sure enough, two wallabies that looked just like them, only not as skinny, were drinking from the river.

"Hello!" shouted Jake, trying to catch their attention.

The wallabies were startled by the sound and looked over at the three ragged strangers.

"Hello!" echoed Peg, waving.

The two wallabies looked at each other, then quickly turned and hopped away.

"That was a bit strange," said Jake.

"And very unfriendly," added Peg.

Wally agreed. "Why do you think they

wouldn't answer back?"

"Who knows?" said Jake. "But they're probably part of a mob. We should try to find them. They might know this area and where the dangers are. Maybe we could even join their mob."

"A mob!" said Peg, hopefully. "Now that would be the cherry on the cake! Imagine not having to worry so much about our safety anymore!"

The thought hung in the air for a moment before she continued, "That's a great idea. Let's go find them and see if they are part of a mob. Maybe they'll let us join."

The words hit Wally with the blunt edge of betrayal. Join another mob? Why would they want to do that? He had led them through all manner of danger, through the Divide and into this lush, green valley. He'd even risked his life for them in the clearing. Why would they suddenly want to dump him for another mob?

The truth was, Wally had grown used to being in charge of his own fate, of not having to answer to anyone, even if it meant bearing the responsibility for the others. Somehow, it gave him a sense of purpose that had been missing in the mob, where wallabies spent their days just lying in the sun. He wasn't sure he wanted to give that up and go back to being just another one of the crowd. The one with the unreliable knee.

"We'll need to find a place to cross," said Jake, as a new plan quickly took shape. "It's a long swim to the other side and, by the way the water's moving, if we start out here, we'll be well downstream by the time we're across. Why don't we head further downstream and look for an easier place to cross?"

"Sounds good," agreed Peg. "Wally?"

"Ah, yes. Sounds good," Wally mumbled half-heartedly, not really thinking about what Jake had said at all.

Jake and Peg bounded back up the bank with enthusiasm. Wally followed behind, still lost in thought. They made their way along the riverbank, following the course of the water, searching for a place to cross.

Jake soon found a narrow section where the river twisted around the landscape. The shallows extended about halfway across, the current fighting its way across a stony riverbed that rippled the surface into whitewater. The easy walk to halfway and the temptation of a short swim to the other side, coupled with Jake's impatience, made it seem like a perfect option, but the shallows of the bend hid the strength of the current in the deeper water.

"This looks better," said Jake, eager not to waste any more time. He stepped into the shallows and began making his way slowly across the river. Peg followed in his footsteps, while

Wally entered a short way downstream.

The shallows quickly gave way to deeper water, and they began to struggle against the force of the current.

"It's moving too quickly, Jake! We should find another place to cross!" shouted Wally over the noise of the river.

"Come on, Wally, we're nearly there!"

Peg was already losing the battle against the current. "Jake, it's getting too deep!"

"Jake!" cried Wally, taking another step into the torrent. "We're not going to make it! The river's flowing too fast! Let's find another place to cross!"

"It's just a few more steps!" Jake insisted, taking one more tentative step.

"Jake!" But before Wally could say any more, the stones under his feet gave way, throwing him off balance. With a great splash, Wally fell into the river and in an instant was swept out into the fast-moving current.

"Wally!" Peg screamed, horrified to see him vanish around the next bend.

She and Jake turned back, battling the current until they reached the safety of the bank, then sprinted along the river's edge, desperately scanning the water for any sign of him.

The river was merciless, tumbling Wally in its

turbulence and slamming him against rocks again and again. He tried to fight his way to the bank, but each time he came close, the river dragged him back. He was swept over rapids, through deep channels, then back into swirling eddies that sucked him under. He bobbed helplessly, struggling to keep his head above the water.

Within minutes, the powerful river had taken its toll. Wally could barely stay afloat as the river drove him around another bend, sweeping him towards the opposite side. Exhausted, he tried to claw his way onto the rocks that broke the surface of the water, but his tiny arms were no match for the strength of the river.

He looked downstream, searching for something to stop his progress, and saw that the river stopped abruptly at the horizon. A thunderous roar filled his ears. That could only mean one thing. A waterfall.

Wally kicked with everything he had left, trying to steer his way to the rocky shelf that extended into the water on the far side. He thrashed through the water, inching closer and closer as the water carried him swiftly towards the falls. He realised he wouldn't make it to the shelf, but he saw a large rock that split the river. If he could get to the other side of the rock, he would be swept closer to the shelf.

He knew this would be his last chance. Fear surged through him as he approached the rock and the water began to accelerate around it. "I will not give in!" he cried, and he lashed out at the river one more time. His foot connected with something hard beneath the swirling water, and as he jammed his foot down, the force of the kick lifted him out of the river, and he flopped ungraciously onto the face of the rock.

The water swirled past him on both sides, hurrying towards the waterfall. Wally, now completely exhausted, dragged himself as far up the rock as he could and collapsed.

* * *

"We've lost him!" cried Peg. She and Jake raced along the bank, eyes darting across the water, hearts pounding. They didn't know if Wally had been swept away or if he'd been trapped under the swirling current.

When they finally arrived at the waterfall, the dread hit them squarely in the chest. There was no sign of Wally. They ran to the edge of the falls, bracing for the sight of his broken body in the water below, but there was no sign of Wally there either.

Peg was frantic. "Where is he?" she cried. "We can't possibly have beaten him!"

"Maybe he grabbed onto something," said Jake.

"Do you think he could still be upriver?" Peg shouted against the roar of the waterfall.

"I don't know," replied Jake, feeling the weight of responsibility pressing on him, shrinking him under his own helplessness. "But if he's not at the bottom of the waterfall, he must be upstream."

"There!" Darcy shouted from the lip of Peg's pouch. "There he is!" He pointed to Wally, collapsed on the rock on the far side of the river.

"Wally!" Peg shouted. "Wally!"

Wally couldn't hear a thing over the deafening waterfall. He wasn't sure what made him open his eyes at that moment, but as he did, he saw his two friends on the other side of the river, waving frantically at him. It was all he could do to raise a paw to let them know he was all right.

"Maybe this was supposed to happen," he thought. "Maybe we need to be separated now."

His tiny arm fell back to the rock with a thud as he finally lost consciousness.

THE TRAIL

Caper picked up Wally's trail on the ridge easily. Tracking the wallabies over the dry, dusty land had been a challenge; the slightest breeze would cover their footprints almost as quickly as they had made them. But now, with the rain turning the dirt to mud, the detail of every footstep was clearly visible in the earth.

He followed Wally's trail down from the ridge and soon found the spot where the three wallabies had reunited.

"They all made it," he realised, horrified to find evidence of all three wallabies. He knew each of them now. The wallaby from the Leap had a distinctive twist in his left foot, likely caused by a weak knee. He was the one responsible for Knuth's death. The other male had a shortened tail, which was obvious in the way his tracks changed when he stood upright. The female's tracks were unremarkable, save for being slightly smaller than the others.

The humiliation of the discovery reignited his frustration. But as his anger flared, he thought of

Knuth. Knuth never wavered. He never succumbed to frustration. He was relentless.

"I must be more like that," Caper told himself. "Especially now that I'm alone. Calm and relentless, like Knuth."

He looked out from the meeting point and was stunned by the richness of the land before him. "So green," he thought. He knew that meant there would be plenty of food. But he wasn't here for that. He was here for those wallabies, and he had already found their trail.

Judging by the trampled grass, the wallabies had stopped to feed. "They can't be far ahead," he thought. How long had it taken the three dingoes to drag the tree across the Divide? A few hours at most.

Caper sniffed at the ground until he found the trail leading away from the meeting point. They were heading to the river. Of course, that made sense.

He looked up at the sky as the night began to close in. Tracking them would have to wait until tomorrow; he didn't want to lose the trail in the dark. He curled up near where the wallabies had met, the scent of the prey still fresh on the ground.

THE LONG WAY AROUND

"Come on, Jake, we have to get over there before Wally rolls off that rock."

Jake and Peg hopped back to the edge of the waterfall, looking down over the drop for a way around it. Beyond the falls, the river widened into a lake, and the current seemed to slow. It was hard to judge from where they stood, but since they hadn't found a crossing upstream, the lake seemed like their only option. The sides of the waterfall were impossibly steep, so they would have to travel inland and take the long way down. If they managed to cross the river, they'd still face a long climb on the other side.

Leaving the river behind, the two wallabies made their way painstakingly through the thick scrub, but after a few dead ends, eventually found a way through the undergrowth and began their descent to the riverbank.

From the bank, the lake stretched wide before them, and they realised the crossing was not going to be as easy as they had hoped. Though the flow of the water had slowed, the current would still pull them downstream if they couldn't swim fast enough to get to the other side before the river narrowed again.

"How are we going to get across here?" Peg asked.

"It's a lot wider than it looked from the top. Let's try further downstream, maybe there's somewhere where we can jump across," Jake suggested hopefully.

After an hour of fruitless searching, it was clear that there was no better way across. Without any other options, they returned to the lake.

"I don't like it," said Peg.

"Neither do I," said Jake. "But what choice do we have? Have you ever swum that far before?"

"I've never even seen that much water!"

"Neither have I, but we can't just stand here. I'm going to see how deep it is."

Jake waded slowly into the water, secretly hoping it would be shallow enough to just walk across.

Peg looked back at the waterfall, half-expecting Wally to be washed over at any minute. They had already wasted too much time, and it was now late afternoon. The urgency began to play on her mind when she noticed the darkness at the edge of the waterfall.

"Hold on, Jake," she said, leaping over to the edge of the waterfall.

Behind the curtain of water, the rock face had been carved out by years of erosion, forming a narrow ledge. The path was wet and slippery, and mist clouded the view into the watery cavern, but it was promising.

She raced back to Jake, who was already half-submerged.

"Jake!" she shouted. "There's a ledge behind the waterfall, we might be able to walk across!"

"What?" said Jake, doubtfully.

"Come on, I'll show you."

Peg led Jake back to the waterfall, and they peered into the misty cavern.

"What do you think?"

"I can't see more than a good hop ahead," said Jake. "It looks risky, but it's worth a shot."

"That's what I was thinking," said Peg, taking her first tentative steps along the ledge.

Peg crept slowly along the slippery path, deafened by the roar of the waterfall. Mist swirled all around her, making it almost impossible to see.

Darcy clung on, his little nose peeking out over the top of Peg's pouch, while Jake shuffled along behind.

The ledge narrowed until Peg could feel the rock wall pressing against her side as she inched ahead. Finally, the path ran out.

"We're going to have to jump through the water!" she yelled.

Jake could barely hear her over the noise of the falling water, but he saw the problem.

"Sorry, for a second there I thought you said we are going to have to jump through the water!"

"We can't be far from the other side now," she called, trying to summon the courage to jump. "If we can just get through the waterfall, it should be a short swim to the bank."

"Well, jump out as hard as you can, Peg," Jake shouted. "If you don't clear the waterfall, the turbulence will hold you under and you'll probably drown."

Peg turned and gave Jake a filthy look.

"Thanks!"

"What if there are rocks out there?" Jake asked.

"Of course there are rocks out there! Just hope you don't hit any! Now back up, so I can get a run up."

She edged back along the ledge until she had enough space for a good bound.

"Okay," she shouted. "See you in a minute!"

"Good luck!" called Jake.

"Darcy! Hold your breath!"

Darcy took a deep breath and disappeared into Peg's pouch. As soon as he was inside, Peg launched herself upwards. As she sailed past the ledge, she twisted her body and kicked against the rock wall with all her strength, hurling herself straight into the torrent.

The water slammed into her as she exploded out the other side. She landed in the lake with a splash and kicked madly to reach the surface. Thankfully, she had been right, the bank was only a short swim away.

She swam as fast as she could, worried for Darcy who was still in her pouch. Finally, her feet touched the bottom, and she scrambled onto the sandy bank. Darcy shot out of her pouch and drew in a breath that seemed far too big for his tiny lungs.

"Are you okay?" Peg asked.

"Yes," Darcy panted. "Fine. A little wet is all."

"Thank heavens," she said breathlessly, looking back just in time to see Jake blast through the wall of water.

She hopped to the river's edge to help him, but Jake was already through the worst of it and soon joined her on the bank.

They looked at each other and suddenly burst out laughing.

"That was intense!" Jake shouted, his eyes wide with excitement.

"Intense is right!" Peg grinned. "You should have seen yourself blast through the waterfall! You must have really kicked off the wall!"

"I was terrified! I couldn't see you, couldn't hear anything, you could have drowned. I was standing behind a giant wall of water, alone, scared out of my wits!"

"Well, you came through like a cannonball," said Peg.

The three of them laughed, then suddenly remembered Wally.

"We're not going to reach him tonight," Jake said. "It's getting dark. We should find somewhere to sleep. We'll get to him in the morning."

"Do you think he'll be all right?" Peg asked.

"I'm sure he'll be fine. As long as he doesn't roll over in his sleep."

Closing In

Caper woke early the next morning and was immediately back on the trail. He tracked the wallabies through the bush with ease, all the way to where they had slept the night before. Judging by the strength of their scent, they were now only a short distance ahead. With his stomach rumbling, he circled the area, then followed their trail across the open field to where they had rested on the grass.

"I must be close now," he thought.

He allowed himself a moment to drink. Carefully scanning the banks for danger, he wandered down to the water's edge, his senses on full alert. The wallabies weren't the only ones who had learned a lesson at Roughneck's Puddle. He lapped at the water cautiously at first, and then greedily. It was the best water he'd tasted in a long time, and a welcome relief from the heat.

"With a water source like this, there should be plenty of food," he thought, as the possibility of ever returning across the Leap began to fade. His makeshift bridge had given him a way home, but now, with plenty of food and water, there was no way he was ever going back to that wasteland.

Wary of letting the wallabies get too far ahead, he turned and followed the trail back up the bank. He tracked them along the river's edge, aware that they were moving quickly now, from the distance between their paw prints.

"I can't let them get away now," he thought, doubling his pace.

Suddenly, the tracks left the bank and headed into the water.

"They've crossed the river," he thought, sniffing the ground for clues. But the tracks soon became confused. As Caper widened his search, it became clear that three wallabies had entered the water slowly, then two had come out at great speed and raced further along the bank.

Where was the third set of tracks, the ones with the twisted left foot? Had they split up? That didn't make sense.

He searched the river and studied the flow. It wasn't an easy place to cross; the current was strong.

"The one from the Leap has fallen in," he realised, "and the other two are chasing him down the river."

"Hopefully he's hurt," Caper thought, noticing the turbulence of the water. "This might be easier than I thought."

He followed the trail along the river all the way to the waterfall, where the tracks became confused again.

"What had happened here?" he wondered. There was confusion in the tracks as they went back and forth along the bank. They must have been searching for him.

"He must have gone over the falls," he thought. "He won't have survived that."

The thought of the wallaby's demise lifted his spirits, though he was disappointed that it had not been by his own hand. But if he had gone over, why did the tracks come back from the waterfall, back upstream?

Caper stood in the footprints of the female, footprints that faced directly across the river. His gaze lifted slowly from the bank and out across the stream of water racing towards the falls.

What had she been looking at?

A moment later, his question was answered.

Lying on a rock on the other side of the river was the wallaby that had confronted Knuth.

A growl rumbled in Caper's throat as he bared his teeth in a murderous grin.

"Not long now, wallaby."

GUS

When Wally finally opened his eyes, it was dark, and the night sky was filled with stars. The sound of the waterfall startled him as he became suddenly aware of where he was. He heaved himself to his feet, his tired and battered body complaining from almost every bone, as the memory of the battle with the river came flooding back. He was covered in scratches and badly bruised, but thankfully, nothing was broken.

The rock he found himself on was flat and tilted gradually into the river, like a giant arrowhead pointing toward the sky. Water swirled around it violently, as if determined to lift the rock into the current and hurl it over the falls.

Wally looked through the darkness to the far bank. Though the moon cast a soft light across the river, he couldn't see any sign of Peg or Jake.

He remembered them waving to him. Had they gone looking for another way across? Even if they had, he couldn't imagine how they could cross such a dangerous river. Maybe they already knew that. Maybe they weren't even trying. He cursed the two strange wallabies they had seen on the opposite bank. If not for them, none of this would have happened. Then he cursed Jake for his impatience.

Loneliness crept up on him then, as he began to wonder if he would ever see his friends again. Divided by the great river and also, it seemed, by their intentions, Wally wondered if this was how things were meant to be. Water, the very thing that had united them on their journey, was now the barrier that separated them, and all for the sake of finding a mob he didn't even want to join. The irony that he was the one on the mob's side of the river only made it worse.

He turned his attention to his side of the river, knowing he had to find a way off the rock. He looked down at the swirling water and tried to judge the distance to the bank in the moonlight.

It would be a fairly easy jump, certainly nothing like the jump at the Leap, but the ordeal with the river had filled him with uncertainty. His body ached, and the isolation had carved a hollow in his confidence.

He moved up the rock, tested his legs, and studied the rocky ledge that formed the nearby bank. The ledge was wet and glistened in the moonlight, but it was impossible to tell if the water covered solid rock or concealed crevices and puddles. "That would make a big difference to the landing," he thought.

Should he wait until daylight? Maybe. But the longer he waited, the more exposed he would become. Any predator that saw him could just wait on the bank, knowing he would have to jump sooner or later.

Wally decided to go while he had the chance. He braced himself, his tired muscles coiling. One good leap, that's all it would take. He launched himself over the churning water and landed safely on the rock platform with a small splash.

"Good jump," said a voice almost beside him.

Wally spun toward the sound, though there was no menace in the voice.

"Who's there?" he demanded in a sharp whisper.

"Just me," said the voice as the owner emerged from the ferns that grew along the bank. Though he was fully grown, the small wallaby was only about half the size of Wally. "I'm Gus."

"You shouldn't sneak up on a bloke like that! You'll give someone a heart attack!" scolded Wally.

"I wasn't really sneaking up on you," Gus replied. "I came down for a drink and saw you on the rock. At first, I wasn't sure if you were alive or not, so I decided to watch you for a while. Seems like a pretty strange place to sleep. Why on earth did you jump out there?"

"I didn't jump out there, I got washed down

the river. My friends and I were trying to cross when I lost my footing and got caught in the current. It's stronger than it looks."

"You were washed down the river? How far?"

"No idea, but it's going to be an awfully long trip back."

"You're lucky you didn't drown."

"I know. I must have hit every rock on the way through, too. By the time the river swung me out of that last bend, I'd had it. It was all I could do to haul myself up on that rock out there."

"Are you hurt?"

"Just bruised, I think. A few scratches. Not too bad really, all things considered."

"So where are your friends now?"

"On the other side of the river, I guess. They might have gone looking for another place to cross, but I don't know where they'll find one. The river's so wide. Maybe I'll have to find a way back over," Wally said, dreading the thought.

"Well, we've had a lot of rain lately. The river is full, it's much wider than usual," Gus said, thoughtfully. "I'm not sure where anyone could cross at the moment. "You might have to wait until the water subsides a little. Or try further upstream, though I don't really know that area well. What made you want to cross in the first place?"

"We saw a couple of wallabies on this side of the river that looked like us. My friends wanted to see if they were part of a mob and if they were, to see if we could join them."

"Hmm," murmured Gus. "I think I know the mob you mean. They look just like you, only not so skinny, right?"

"Yes," replied Wally.

"And they're about a day's hop upstream from here?"

"More or less, I suppose, at least that's where we saw them. Do you know them?"

"I know of them," replied Gus. "But I can't say I know much about them. There's been some trouble in that area. The crows have been cawing about it, but I'm not sure what kind.

"Anyway, you look pretty banged up," he added. "Why don't you come back to my place and rest for the night? You'll be able to see the riverbank from there, in case your friends find their way across and come looking for you."

"That would be great," Wally said, relieved at the thought of a safe place to rest.

He followed Gus up a narrow track that wound its way into the hills beside the river. The trail led to a space at the end of a curved walkway that ran between two large boulders. A large rock formed an overhang at the end of the path that provided shelter. The den was well hidden, dry, and although the waterfall was quite close, the noise seemed so distant inside the den that it was almost soothing.

Inside, Wally was met by two echidnas whose spines rattled at the sight of him.

"It's all right, you two," said Gus. "This poor bloke's just been washed down the river. He's going to rest here for the night. This is Needles, and this is Pins," he said, introducing the two echidnas to Wally. "I don't think I caught your name..."

"Wally. Pleased to meet you."

"Oh, you won't get much conversation out of them," Gus smiled, "but they do a wonderful job of keeping the den free of ants."

Wally wondered why a wallaby would be sharing his den with a couple of echidnas, but he kept the thought to himself.

"So if you're not from the mob that lives up the river, where are you from?" Gus asked as he and Wally settled down on the floor of the den.

"We came from a place a long way west of here," said Wally. "Through the Divide. It might sound strange if you live here, but our mob was starving. It hadn't rained in a long time and if you could find something to eat, it was dry and tasteless. The commander didn't want to move the mob on, so the three of us decided to leave. Of course, once we'd left, we knew we couldn't go back. Then some dingoes found us..."

Wally went on, telling the story of their journey while Gus, Needles, and Pins listened intently.

"We couldn't believe it when we got here," Wally continued. "The land was so green. And to see such a huge river, with plenty of water..." His words trailed off as he remembered the scene at the top of the Divide.

"It's a beautiful place, there's no question about that," said Gus. "But was it worth it? Giving up your mob like that."

"Absolutely," Wally replied, surprised by the question. "Starvation is not exactly pleasant."

The words hung in the air awkwardly until Wally filled the silence.

"So, what about you?" he asked. "You don't have a mob either."

"No, I don't have a mob," Gus admitted, "but not for want of one. I belonged to the northernmost mob of Parma wallabies. We were a strong mob, until one year a strange-looking creature appeared. Orange fur with a thick bushy tail. Smaller than a dingo, but with very sharp teeth inside a long, pointy jaw and so cunning! That horrible animal terrorised our mob. We tried to keep moving, but he always seemed to find us. One by one, he took us, until I was the last one left. I started searching for another mob, or at least to warn them of what was coming.

Night after night I would zigzag across the

land. I didn't find a single Parma, but I did see more of those horrible orange creatures."

"Finally, I arrived here, alone. There are no more Parmas left, Wally. If I'm not the last, I reckon I'm pretty close."

Gus paused for a moment as he tried to come to terms with what he had just said. He had never spoken of his search before, and the finality of it darkened him.

"You know, it might seem a little strange that a wallaby is sharing his den with a couple of echidnas, but they've been very obliging and they're great company for me. So I'm happy to stay here with them," he said, casting a smile over to Needles and Pins.

"You mean you've given up looking for a mob?" Wally asked.

"You can call it that, but I've tried everything. I've searched everywhere and now I'm too old to be tearing around the countryside. I feel like I've covered just about every inch of the entire east coast, and I'm tired of searching for something I may never find."

To Wally, that sounded like giving up. But he wondered what his own life would be like, if he was left all by himself. He didn't want to settle down like Gus, but the thought of a solitary life struck him harder than he was expecting. Was he searching for something that *he'd* never find?

"I'm happy here, Wally," Gus continued. "I've

got the river just down the hill, I've got plenty to eat, a warm place to sleep, and two good mates. That's all I need right now."

Two good mates. Wally thought that over and wondered where Peg and Jake were. Surely they hadn't abandoned him, not after all they'd been through. Wally cast the doubts aside. They were probably trying to find their way across the river right now, and when they did eventually find him, he'd go with them to find the other wallabies. He could always tear off on his own if he didn't like the new mob. He'd already been banished once, what difference would it make if he was banished again?

Wally and Gus traded stories of their travels into the early hours of the morning, until Wally, unable to keep his eyes open any longer, finally drifted off into a deep, peaceful sleep.

Search

Jake and Peg woke early the next morning and immediately set off, winding their way through the bush and back up the other side of the waterfall. By the time they reached the top, the best part of the morning was gone, and they were both breathing heavily from the exertion. They hopped along the bank to the rock where they had last seen Wally, only to find he was gone.

"Wally!" cried Peg, but the sound was quickly swallowed by the sound of the waterfall. "Where is he, Jake? Do you think he fell in?"

"He could have made the jump from that rock. It's not that far. I'm sure he'll be all right," said Jake, but Peg could hear the uncertainty in his voice.

"He looked pretty beaten up to me. If he's fallen in..."

"Come on, Peg. He'll be all right. We'll have a look around here, and if we can't find him, we'll go back and search down the river again."

"Oh, Jake! He could be anywhere by now!"

Visions of a lifeless Wally crushed by the power of the waterfall filled Peg's mind. How could they have come this far just to lose him like this? "If only you hadn't tried to force your way across the river!"

"I didn't know the water would be running that fast," Jake replied defensively. "It seemed okay where I was."

"Wally!" Peg cried again, but it was useless, and she knew it.

Jake started to search the shore for a sign that Wally had made the jump from the rock. There were no clues on the rock shelf, but as he widened his search, he found a small trail leading up the hill. On the trail, barely visible, were two sets of footprints, one belonging to a wallaby about Wally's size, and the other to a much smaller wallaby.

"Peg! Peg!" he called. "I think I've found something!"

"Do you think these are Wally's?" he asked hopefully as Peg joined him.

"Yes!" exclaimed Peg. "Look at the angle of the left foot. That's Wally for sure!"

Peg was suddenly filled with hope. He was alive and on the shore. Now all they had to do was find him.

The Gathering

It was late in the morning when Needles wandered back into the den and woke Gus to let him know about the two wallabies at the river.

"Wally," Gus said, waking him gently, "it looks like your friends have arrived."

Wally immediately jumped to his feet, but the stiffness in his limbs reminded him of the previous day's ordeal. He hopped gingerly to the front of the den and, just as Gus had said, had a clear view down to the river. He spotted Jake and Peg hopping along the bank, looking agitated and confused. They had obviously discovered that he was no longer on the rock.

"I'd better go, Gus. They must think I've fallen in. Thanks for putting me up last night."

"No worries, Wally. Stop by anytime. I enjoyed our chat."

"So did I," Wally called over his shoulder as he bounded down the hill to meet his friends.

Peg had followed the trail of footprints, and

as she looked further up the hill, she saw a familiar face making its way down.

"Wally!"

She hopped up the hill and scolded him. "You had me worried sick, Wally! I thought you'd gone over the waterfall! Could you have at least left a signal or something?"

"Oh, sure," Wally replied with a smile. "Maybe I should've left a 'Tasty Wallaby This Way' sign with an arrow on the bank. Sorry, Peg. I didn't know how long you two would be, or if you were even coming, and I didn't want to be sitting out in the open."

"Of course we were coming! What were you thinking? Thank heavens you're all right."

"*Are* you all right?" asked Jake. "It looked like you took quite a beating coming down that river."

"I sure did, but luckily it's just bruises," Wally replied. "I'll be fine. But how on earth did you cross the river?"

"It took us forever," Jake said. "It's a long way down on the far side of the waterfall, and the current was still flowing pretty quickly when we finally got there. But once we reached the bank, Peg found a ledge behind the falls. We could walk most of the way across. Then we had to jump through the waterfall because the ledge ran out."

"You jumped through a waterfall?" Wally asked in disbelief.

Peg turned to Jake and they both started laughing at the madness of what they had done.

"Then we had to swim ashore, and it was a decent climb to get back up the hill to the top of the waterfall on this side. But we made it, I'm happy to say."

"Well, I'm glad you're both all right. Did you see any sign of dingoes on your way across?"

"We didn't really think about that," admitted Jake, glancing at Peg. "We just found a place to sleep and came up as fast as we could. How about you?"

"I was fine. I met a little Parma wallaby named Gus. He let me stay in his den with his two echidnas."

Jake and Peg looked at each other as though Wally had lost his mind.

"Are you sure you didn't cop a knock to the head on the way down the river?" asked Jake.

"No, I'm fine! Really! I can take you up and you can see for yourself."

"Sure, mate. Whatever you say," Jake replied. "But let's save that for another time. If you're feeling okay, we'd best get moving, the day's getting away from us. Now that we've found you, we'd better start looking for that mob."

As soon as the words left Jake's mouth, Wally felt his heart sink. Jake turned and leapt away, with Peg close behind. Wally hesitated and watched them for a moment, then reluctantly followed.

They made good progress as they travelled back upstream. The grass was low, and they could easily follow the river by the gum trees lining the bank. They tried to recognize some of the trees that they had passed on the opposite bank to figure out where they were, but all the trees seemed to look the same. An argument soon broke out as to whether they'd gone too far or not far enough. None of them had thought to look for a landmark in their haste to cross the river.

"All these trees look the same," Jake said.

"That's because they are all the same!" said an irritated Peg. "The other side looks so different from this side, and nothing like I remember it when we were on that side. How is that possible?"

"The other side always looks different," Wally said. "We must be getting close now. Isn't that the tree where we first stopped for a drink?"

"No," Jake said. "It didn't look anything like that!"

"It looked exactly like that!"

The bickering woke Darcy, who had been asleep in Peg's pouch. He peeked out into the daylight.

"Hey, can you keep it down? I'm trying to sleep."

"Maybe you should get out of that pouch and

help us look," Jake snapped, tired of the search. "We can't find the spot where we saw those other two wallabies. Every tree looks the same."

"They all look pretty different to me," said Darcy, having spent most of his life in trees. "You're way off. It was much further upstream where we saw those wallabies."

"How can you tell?" asked Jake.

"I remember the trees," Darcy said. "You want to spend more time watching where you're going, Jake. Keep going upriver. You've got a way to go yet."

They turned and continued further up the river, now under Darcy's expert guidance.

"There," he said finally. "That's the tree where we first stopped at the bank."

"Yes, that's it. It looks very familiar now," said Peg.

"I guess I remember that tree now," said Wally, not sure how that tree looked any different from the hundreds they'd just passed.

"Looks exactly the same as all the others to me." How Darcy could tell one from another still baffled Jake.

They hopped down to the bank and began looking for the other wallabies' footprints. It wasn't long before Peg had found them in the soft mud.

"Here!" she cried, excited by the discovery.

Wally and Jake joined her, and they all agreed the tracks were fresh. They followed the trail from the mud up into the grass, where it disappeared into more thick scrub. Pushing their way through the bush, they eventually emerged a short distance from a large rocky hill that rose out of the landscape, speckled with wallabies.

"That must be it," said Wally. "What do you think?"

"Looks good to me," Jake said. "Elevated, good for spotting anything coming, yet open enough to escape. Though I don't fancy sleeping on those rocks."

"I'm sure you'll be able to find somewhere to sleep," said Wally. "What do you think, Peg?"

"Looks great! There's plenty of space, it's close to the river, and there's more grass than we could eat in a hundred years. Another mob! I can't wait to meet them!"

"Let's not get too far ahead of ourselves," said Wally, his reluctance beginning to surface again.

He had an uneasy feeling that his brief encounter with freedom was about to come to an abrupt end.

WATERFALL

Caper knew he couldn't cross the river directly, but he was certain the other two wallabies would be trying to find a way to the other side. He found the trail Jake and Peg had left as they made their way toward the base of the waterfall and followed it until nightfall. Tired, he settled in for the night, the distant sound of the waterfall lulling him to sleep, unaware that Jake and Peg were sleeping just across the river.

In the morning, Caper followed the tracks all the way to the sandy bank at the bottom of the waterfall, where once again the tracks became confused and scattered. The wallabies had been searching for something, but were unsure where to find it. He followed the tracks as far as they went downstream, only to find them stop and double back to the waterfall.

"Back to the waterfall?" he thought. "They must have decided to swim across at the lake." But he could only find one set of footprints leading into the water.

He surveyed the lake, and the same thought

went through his mind as had gone through Jake's and Peg's. It was a long way across, and the current was still flowing quickly.

"I've missed something," he thought, puzzled by the trail. He searched the bank again and found the two sets of footprints leading to the waterfall.

"That must be a dead end," he assumed, but with no other clues, he followed the tracks to the waterfall and saw that both sets of footprints went in, and none came out. He scanned the sand for a trail leading off the rocks, and then he saw the ledge.

He stepped closer and peered into the misty cavern behind the waterfall. "Wow," he said aloud, impressed by the wallabies' courage. They must have walked along the ledge behind the falls. Cautiously, he stepped up onto the narrow ledge and disappeared behind the curtain of water.

The noise was deafening. Torrents of water fell from above and thundered into the lake. The air was thick with a mist that clouded Caper's vision. He inched his way forward, stepping carefully along the wet rock, until he arrived at the end of the ledge.

"This is madness!" he thought. Had they really jumped through the waterfall? Surely not. He searched for an alternative, but knew there wasn't one. If he was going to follow them, he'd have to jump too.

He stared into the violence of the falls, and the

danger made him hesitate. Maybe he should just go out and swim across, despite the speed of the current. He wondered how far he would be carried downstream, and whether he could even swim that distance.

Suddenly, his impatience took a firm hand.

"Oh, for heaven's sake! If those wallabies can do it, then so can I."

He backed up slowly along the ledge to get a good run-up, then sprinted along the ledge and hurled himself into the falls.

The force of the water hit him like a sledgehammer, driving him deep into the lake. Unlike Jake and Peg, who had kicked off the rock wall with enough force to send them through the waterfall, Caper had just leapt off the ledge and was immediately pounded into the churning waters.

He thrashed at the water, trying to right himself, the water rolling him over and over until he had no idea which way was up. Minutes seemed to last forever as a thousand currents held him down and the last bubbles of breath left his shrinking lungs. Then, in one great surge, he was drawn back under the impact zone and thrust out into the lake.

His nose broke the surface and he gasped for air, only to be dragged under again. He felt the turbulence losing its grip on him as he whipped his paws through the whitewater. Again he broke the surface and caught another lungful of precious air. This time, he managed to keep his head above the surface and swim clear of the falls.

Weakened from the beating, he found himself being swept downstream by the current. He swam desperately for the shore, his muscles aching with exhaustion, his lungs heaving for air. Finally, his paws struck the bottom. He hauled himself out of the water and collapsed on the sandy bank.

"I should have just tried to swim across," he murmured, regretting every moment of the leap into the falls.

A sheer cliff towered above him, preventing his movement back upstream, and as he looked back towards the waterfall, now a long way in the distance, a single thought struck him as he surrendered to his tiredness.

He had lost the trail.

THE MOB

The hill rose out of the landscape like an afterthought from the creation of the mountains behind it. Isolated from the range, it was surrounded by open grassy fields and covered in rocks and stones. A few tall gum trees stood on the western side, and well-worn trails crisscrossed its face. It seemed a perfect location for a mob: the elevation offered a clear view over the countryside, the rocks provided shelter from the elements, and the tracks between the rocks allowed for a quick escape if necessary. With the river close by, it all seemed too good to be true.

The three wallabies approached slowly to avoid startling the mob, but it became clear that the mob had seen them coming and were already gathering in anticipation of their arrival.

More and more wallabies emerged as they drew near, until the rocky hill was covered with them, all watching intently as the trio crossed the field that separated them from the mob. The mob was well fed; there wasn't a lean wallaby among them.

"Kind of spooky, don't you think?" asked Wally.

Peg sensed it too. "Yeah, something weird is going on."

"Here we go again," said Jake. "Stop worrying, will you? They're probably just not used to stray wallabies wandering in. It's a big mob, every wallaby within cooee must be here."

"That's the strange thing," Wally replied. "Why would so many wallabies gather here? We haven't seen any other mobs while we've been here, or even found evidence of other mobs. And why would so many come out just to watch us arrive?" said Wally. "I'm with Peg, this feels odd."

"Oh, you're both a pair of worrywarts," Jake scoffed. "This place couldn't be more perfect. Look at the layout, it's ideal. Maybe that's why there are so many here; everyone loves the place."

"Hmm," said Wally. "We'll see." As they approached the base of the hill, he looked up and called out, "Hello!"

They could feel the eyes of a hundred wallabies on them, but not a single one responded.

Confused, the trio stopped. Wally repeated his greeting.

Slowly, in front and some height above them, three members of the mob emerged and took their position on a large rock that jutted out from the hill like a giant stage. Wally could tell immediately that one of them was the mob commander. He was older than the other two and wore the air of importance. His fur was marked by a long white streak down his right flank, and the grim look on his face was anything but welcoming.

On the commander's right stood a nasty-looking wallaby, with tiny black eyes that struggled to see through a natural squint. His body was bent over in a permanent hunch, and he wrung his paws constantly.

The third wallaby was enormous, almost the size of a kangaroo, with strong, powerful legs that looked capable of kicking a wallaby clear across the river. He towered over the others and was easily the largest wallaby Wally had ever seen.

"Hello," Wally called again, this time more respectfully.

It wasn't until the commander had looked over Jake, Peg, and Wally that he finally spoke. "What do you want?" he asked, without a trace of hospitality.

"We're looking for a mob, a place to settle down. We saw two wallabies down by the river..."

"Where are you from?" the commander demanded.

"We've come from the west, our mob was starving."

"From the west?" the commander interrupted again. "This is the west. You're not from around here."

"No, we're not," Wally said. "We travelled through the dry lands west of the Divide. We managed to cross it and arrived here."

That drew a rumble of disbelief from the mob.

"You crossed the Divide, did you?"

"Yes."

"Humph," the commander grunted, as though it was the most ridiculous thing he'd ever heard. "And now you want to join our mob. Is that it?"

"Yes."

Wally was taken aback by the commander's hostility. He hadn't expected a reception like this, in fact, quite the opposite. He had assumed they would be welcome in a mob that seemed to have an abundance of everything.

"If it's not too much trouble," he added.

"Trouble?" the commander sneered. "You wander in here, three of the skinniest, most sickly-looking wallabies I've ever seen, with some ridiculous story about crossing the Divide, having deserted your own mob, and you expect to be welcomed? No wallaby has ever crossed the Divide, let alone three that looked like you."

"Well, we did," Wally said firmly. "Jake and Peg came up through the boulders, and I crossed the Leap."

"You crossed the Leap, did you?" mocked the commander. "Everyone knows that gap is too wide for a wallaby. And you're telling me that somehow, a skinny little wallaby with an obvious problem with his leg managed to clear it? A feat beyond even the most graceful of wallabies. I wish I'd been there to see that."

"So do I," Wally replied sharply, the mention of his knee stirring a spike of resentment. He'd thought his leg was getting better. He knew it was. There had been far fewer misfires lately. How had the commander noticed?

Wally let his temper get the better of him and went on the offensive. "I can certainly imagine someone as stout as you would have trouble with the Leap. But we're fit, though we may not look it. We were chased by a pack of dingoes almost the whole way. You'll find one of them at the bottom of the Leap if you'd care to take a look."

"Don't waste my time, son. No wallaby has made it through the Divide, and there's no way you three mangy creatures would be the first."

Peg stepped alongside Wally and spoke. "Look, we seem to have gotten off on the wrong foot. We don't mean to put you out. We were just looking for a place to stay, a mob to join. We're not asking for anything more than that. Does it really matter how we got here?"

"It does to me," said the commander. "You

deserted your own mob. Then you turn up here with some far-fetched tale of crossing the Divide, and I'm supposed to trust you? How do I know you're not sick? You don't look too healthy to me, so why would I risk the health of the mob by taking you in?"

"We were starving!" replied Peg, exasperated by the questioning. "It's not like this out west. You don't understand. There's no food, there's no water. If anything, we helped our mob by leaving because without us, there were fewer mouths to feed."

"There's not a mob alive that would believe that story. You left your mob. You broke the wallaby code. That's all there is to it."

"Wait, just a moment," said the wallaby with the dark eyes, his words curling around his tongue. "Let's not be too hasty. We're all wallabies here, aren't we? Perhaps we can come to some arrangement. Commander, may I have a word?"

He and the commander turned away and spoke in a low whisper the others couldn't hear. After a few moments, the commander turned back to Wally and spoke.

"All right," he started, "Mennas has persuaded me to give you a chance. You are wallabies, after all, our own kind, more or less," he added scornfully. "But you'll have to stay in the rock pit until we are sure that you're not carrying some kind of disease."

Wally turned to Jake and Peg. "I'm against this. This bloke sounds worse than our old commander. What do you two think?"

Peg looked to Jake, who shrugged. "It's a big mob. I'm sure they're not all like him. How about we give it a chance?"

Peg agreed.

Wally nodded reluctantly. Against his better judgement, he turned back to the commander. "That's fine, thank you. You'll soon see there's nothing wrong with us."

"All right. Doogan, take them up to the rock pit," the commander ordered.

The giant wallaby stepped forward and tipped his head as if to say 'Follow me'. Wally, Peg, and Jake followed him up into the rocks, beneath the stares and whispers of the rest of the mob. If the commander's intention was to make them feel like outcasts, it was working.

They climbed to the outer edge of the mob's territory, arriving at a natural stone bowl set into the side of the hill. It was big enough to hold about a dozen wallabies. There was no shade and no grass. There was only one way into the bowl, and the walls were too steep to jump over. It looked like a natural prison.

"There you go, your new home. Welcome to Rocky Hill," Doogan said flatly, before bounding back down the path.

"The nerve of that commander!" said Peg once Doogan was out of earshot. "Fancy treating us like that! We would never have greeted strangers like that in our old mob!"

"I didn't like it either," Jake agreed, "but what else are we going to do? And I suppose we do look pretty sickly," eyeing the bones that lined their fur. "I'd probably be suspicious of us too. You know, when you say it out loud, our story does sound a bit fanciful. Three wallabies cross a huge expanse of barren wasteland and then cross a seemingly impenetrable Divide. That happens all the time, right?" he said light-heartedly. "Anyway, a week or two here and we'll be as chubby as they are. They'll come around, I'm sure. But I can't say I'm too impressed with our accommodation. Is this really the best room they had available?"

Wally was still fuming at the commander's welcome and was in no mood for jokes. "Hopefully we won't be here for long," he muttered. Then he remembered the commander's comments about his knee.

"Hey," he started, self-consciously, "is my leg still that obvious?"

"What?" Jake was surprised by the sudden change of subject.

"My leg. It feels like it's much better to me, but the commander picked it straight away. Is it still that obvious?"

"I didn't know you were trying to hide it," said

Peg. "Or that you were that worried about how it looked."

"I'm not trying to hide it," Wally replied, a little defensively, "I just thought it was getting better, so maybe it was less noticeable."

"If you mean can we recognise you when you hop across a field, then yes, we can tell it's you. Your hop is kind of unique."

"There's only one wallaby who jumps like you, Wally, and that's you," Jake added with a smile. "You're one of a kind. I just wish you'd do more acrobatics. I kind of miss them."

"Yeah, especially those backflips," agreed Peg. "Those were awesome when you nailed them. Maybe you could teach me how to do that someday."

"Well, here's how I do it," Wally replied. "Just hop along for a while and see what happens. I couldn't do that on purpose if I wanted to, it's completely involuntary. I just hope my feet hit the ground before my face does."

That brought a laugh from Jake and Peg, and the trio's spirits began to lift. After some more good-natured ribbing, the wallabies decided to rest in the afternoon heat. They found a little shade where the highest rocks were blocking the sun, but struggled to find comfort on the hard, rock floor.

Wally couldn't help but feel uneasy. They'd suddenly gone from the freedom of their little band to being governed by another strict mob commander who had insisted they stay on as outcasts, away from the rest of the mob.

"I hope we won't be all the way up here for long," he thought. "We're so isolated that we might as well be on our own." But he couldn't deny it, there was some relief in being back behind the eyes of a large mob, with the security and protection they provided. It would be so easy to believe that this was where they could finally settle down, but something just didn't feel right. And Peg had felt it too.

Maybe he was just overreacting. Maybe they just needed time to get to know the mob. Then again, maybe his head was just trying to turn down the volume on what his gut was saying, loud and clear.

ALLIANCE

Caper woke with a start, quickly remembering where he was and what he should have been doing. He wondered how long he had slept, how much time had passed, how much more distance the wallabies had put between them and him.

Cursing himself, he jumped to his feet and immediately felt a pair of eyes watching him. He raised his head slowly and turned to confront the animal.

Sitting casually on a large rock a short way up the hill was an animal that was unfamiliar to Caper. Smaller than a dingo and more orange in colour, the animal was clearly a hunter. Its long snout was lined with sharp teeth, and its eyes pointed forward. It could have passed for a small, delicate dingo if not for its oversized ears and the long, bushy tail that waved slowly in the air.

"Where's your pack, lonesome?"

"Who are you?" Caper demanded. The last thing he wanted was competition for the wallabies. "Or should I ask, what are you?"

"Shar is my name," the animal replied confidently. "And though I've been called many things, I am actually a common fox. Although, I'd like to think not too common, if I may be so bold. So tell me, friend, what is a lone dingo doing all the way out here?"

Shar's keen eye had seen everything, Wally's fortune at the rock, the pair of wallabies crossing the river, and finally the movements of the dingo, who was obviously tracking the wallabies. Caper's performance at the waterfall had been especially entertaining, but despite the amusement, the sight of a solitary dingo was unusual, and Shar saw the opportunity immediately.

"I'm tracking three wallabies," Caper said defiantly.

"Why just three?" Shar asked. "There's a whole mob up the river."

"I've got a score to settle with them. I don't suppose you've seen three wallabies pass through here?"

"Perhaps," Shar said carefully. "I've seen many wallabies around here. I couldn't be certain they're the ones you're after, though. What did they look like?"

"Greyish-brown, like normal wallabies I suppose, just thinner. I saw one of them lying on a rock above the waterfall and, from their tracks, the other two crossed the river below the waterfall, like I did."

"Oh, they managed it a lot more gracefully than you did," Shar thought to himself, smiling.

"Yes, yes! I did see two wallabies come through here. Grey and emaciated they were, looked like they could use a good meal. They slept the night not far from here. They've gone back upstream, perhaps they went looking for their friend."

"Good," said Caper. "Then I'd better get back on the trail. I don't want to lose them."

"But you'll need a pack for that, won't you? I'm afraid the nearest dingoes are quite a long way away."

"I don't need a pack," said Caper. "Not for what I intend to do."

"Oh, every dingo needs a pack!" insisted Shar. "I've seen you fellows operate. You're not that fast, so you surround your prey and corner them. You can't surround anything if there's just one of you, can you? How will you gang up on your prey without a pack?"

"I do just fine by myself," replied Caper, becoming annoyed at the fox's cheekiness.

"Well, I don't mean to be rude, but it doesn't look like it. Look how skinny you are. I can see your bones! You haven't had a good feed in weeks, have you? A bit strange, if you don't mind me saying. There's plenty to eat around here. Perhaps you should find yourself a pack."

The thought played at Caper's mind. He hadn't had a proper meal in a long time, just scraps the pack had found along the way while chasing those blasted wallabies. If the truth were told, he was starving.

"But maybe there's more to it than that," Shar mused. "You seem like a pretty smart fellow. I don't think you want to be just another dingo in a pack, do you? You're ready to be the leader. But you'll need more than brains for that. A leader has to be the strongest, and to be quite blunt, you're not that big. For a dingo, I mean. What if you could find something smaller for your pack? Something like me, for instance?"

"Like you? You're not even a dingo! I don't need a fancy little upstart like you in my pack."

"Oh, but you do! You do! With your sharp intellect and my cunning, we'd be unstoppable, don't you think? I'm quite the hunter, you know."

"You? What do you hunt? Mice? Forget it. It would look ridiculous having you in my pack. How can it be a pack of dingoes if some of the animals in the pack aren't even dingoes?"

"Oh, nonsense!" replied the fox. "It's just something you haven't seen before. Be the first! Be the innovator! I'd be honoured to be a member of your pack. We'd make a great team, the two of us. I'll tell you what, why don't we have a little hunting party tonight and see if we can't find you something to eat? You'll need your strength to catch those wallabies. If it works out, you'll get a good meal. If not, you're really no worse off, are you? You can always pick up the wallabies' trail again. Besides, I may be able to help you find them."

Caper thought about the fox's idea. It seemed to make sense, and besides, what did he have to lose? Maybe a few hours at worst. And if they did catch something, maybe it would finally silence the incessant rumbling in his stomach. And if the fox really could help him find the wallabies...

"What's in it for you?" he asked suspiciously.

"For me?" Shar answered, pretending to be surprised. "The prestige! The honour! How many foxes do you see running with a dingo pack? I'll be the first, with you as my leader. Two hunters are better than one, right?"

That was certainly how Caper saw the world. Prey was easier to round up when there was more than one hunter. Alone, it was always just a chase. Though he still felt uneasy about the arrangement, the temptation of a good meal was irresistible.

"So, what did you have in mind?" he asked.

"Just a little hunting trip. There's quite a bit of game in the hills behind me, and it's ours for the taking. Why don't we meet here at dusk and see how well we work together?"

Caper couldn't think of a good reason not to.

He knew he would need to be in good condition when he finally faced the wallabies. Their trail had covered a lot more ground than he had expected, and after the ordeal with the waterfall, he decided to take his chances with the fox.

"All right," he said finally. "I'll see you here at dusk."

* * *

Caper lay in the sun for the rest of the afternoon, dozing off while the sun warmed his skin. When he woke late that afternoon, Shar was already waiting.

"Hello, sleepyhead," he said. "Did you have a pleasant nap?"

"I did," Caper replied, embarrassed to have been so lazy. "How long have you been there?"

"I just got here." The lie slid off Shar's tongue like butter off a hot knife. He had been watching Caper for most of the afternoon, while his plan began to develop in his mind.

"Are you ready for some supper?" he asked, as though finding food would be the easiest thing in the world.

"More than ready. Where are we going?" Caper asked bluntly, wary of the fox's confidence.

"There's a flock of bush turkeys not far from here. I'm sure we could nab one or two. I know they're not the most tender of the bushland meats, but it's a start."

Tender or not, Caper was already salivating at the thought of the meal. "Okay," he said. "Lead the way."

Shar led him up the hill and through a tangle of undergrowth. The going was tough, at least for Caper, but the fox seemed to slip through the brush easily, darting through the smallest of gaps. Caper battled through the worst of it until the bush thinned out, reducing their cover.

"Keep quiet!" whispered Shar, astonished at the racket the dingo was making. "We'll never catch anything with you stomping around like that! No wonder you're hungry!"

Caper tried to tread more lightly, but he seemed to snap a twig with every step, much to Shar's disgust. This wasn't how Caper had been taught to hunt.

"They'll be around here somewhere," whispered the fox.

Suddenly Shar stopped. Caper stopped immediately, with an audible crack from yet another twig.

"There they are," the fox whispered, as four large bush turkeys appeared in front of them. "Perfect. I'll circle around behind them. Give me a minute or two, and then start herding them over to that rock. I'll be behind it. Hopefully, we'll catch one by surprise. Whatever you do, don't move too quickly or you'll frighten them and they'll fly into the trees. Got it?"

"Got it," Caper affirmed, his stomach growling at the thought of the meal.

Any reservations he had about the fox were fading quickly. Caper waited for the fox to get in position, then began moving forward slowly. Despite his hunger, he resisted the urge to rush at the turkeys and gradually began to herd them towards the rock. The turkeys saw Caper but didn't seem too concerned, as long as he kept his distance. He continued to stalk the turkeys, moving them closer to the rock.

"Come on!" he thought. "What is he waiting for?" The turkeys were close now, and any scent of the fox would spook them.

Caper's patience started to falter. "I can't keep this up much longer," he thought. "They're getting agitated. They can feel themselves getting cornered."

Should he just rush them now? Surely he could get one of them.

"Patience," he told himself again, as he continued to work the turkeys back.

The turkeys' eyes were locked on Caper's every move.

Suddenly, Shar burst out from behind the rock. In two lightning-quick steps, he caught a turkey from behind and wrestled it to the ground. Caper rushed in to help as the other turkeys flew off into the trees.

"For you, my leader," said Shar, presenting Caper with the bird.

Caper looked at him. "Yes. This is how things should be," he thought. "Who cares what's in my pack, as long as they can hunt? This will do nicely."

Caper tore a leg off the turkey and gave it to the fox. "Joint effort," he said.

"I must say, that was easy. We make an excellent team," Shar replied respectfully.

Caper barely heard him. He tore into the turkey with ravenous abandon. Bones, meat, and gizzards were all wolfed down, and soon the air was filled with feathers. It was the best meal he'd had in weeks. His belly full and the taste of the prey dripping off his lips, Caper leaned back, satisfied.

"That was good."

"Yes," replied Shar, surprised by the savagery as he delicately picked his turkey leg clean. "A bit chewy and not nearly as juicy as kangaroo or wallaby, but not bad all the same."

"Oh, wouldn't I love to sink my teeth into a wallaby," said Caper, the image of the three wallabies suddenly vivid in his mind.

"I think I can help you with that," said Shar. "I know which way they went. They shouldn't be too hard to find."

Blinded by the prospect of finding the three wallabies, Caper sealed the deal. "When do we start?"

"In the morning," said Shar. "It's a fair walk to the top of the waterfall through the hills, but there's no point in waiting, is there?"

"Okay. Tomorrow morning. Early."

"Of course," replied Shar. "Whatever you wish, chief. But now I need to return to my den. I don't sleep out in the open like you. I'll see you here, bright and early." He waited for Caper's nod, then trotted off into the hills.

"That was all too easy," he thought to himself.

COMMANDER

"Okay, Mennas. This plan you have for the three blow-ins, let's hear it."

"The wallaby with the bad knee gave me the idea," replied Mennas. "You and I both know the dogs will be back in a matter of days, and that means some of us are going to die, probably the joeys again."

"Yes, yes, we've been through all this before. So what?" said the commander, irritated by the inevitable return of the wild dogs and his inability to stop their raids. It happened almost like clockwork: a scourge of dogs, far worse than dingoes, came in from the north, attacked the mob, and left with the weak and the small.

The dogs had terrorised every mob in the area until they had all gradually made their way to his. He'd taken them all in, believing that there was strength in numbers, that more eyes would improve their safety. But instead, he had unwittingly focused all the dogs' attention on a single, large mob. A concentrated group made for an easier hunt, and the dogs kept coming back, again and again.

He felt powerless to stop them now. Moving would mean giving up the rocky shelter, and the dogs would only track them anyway. As much as he hated to admit it, he had resigned himself to the attack. All he could do was prepare for it, promising safety he knew he couldn't deliver, knowing that the mob would eventually succumb to the dogs.

"We have few enough joeys left, Commander. As a mob, we're shrinking. We can't afford to lose any more."

"I don't need a lesson on predators, Mennas," the commander replied flatly. He knew well enough that the joeys were the key to the mob's future.

"Well, what if the children weren't the weakest among us?" Mennas asked.

"What do you mean?"

"What if the three strangers were the easiest prey?"

"They don't look that weak to me," replied the commander. "Skinny, yes, but they all seem pretty robust. Especially that one with half a tail."

"They may look able enough now, perhaps, but what if that wasn't the case? One already has a malformed knee. What if they all had weak knees or, better yet, broken knees?"

"You want to break their legs?" The

commander was shocked by the suggestion.

"Why not? They're not part of our mob. They've blown in from who knows where, and they already look sickly. No one would suspect anything, and the dogs would be all over them."

The brutality of the plan horrified the commander. But the mob had lost so many joeys, and he had to find a way to stop it. He looked sternly at Mennas. "You would sacrifice your own kind?"

"My kind? Let's not forget, Commander, it was they who came to us. It's your duty to protect the mob at all costs. We know nothing about these three wallabies. They may even be a danger to us. They arrived with an impossible story about crossing the Divide, which we both know isn't true. They're liars.

"This is an opportunity you must take, for the good of the mob."

"And how, exactly, do you suggest we do this?"

"We keep them in the rock pit until tomorrow night. Then we send Doogan in after dark while they're asleep. He only needs to jump on their legs, one after the other. It will all be over in a matter of seconds. Then we drag them into the open. When the dogs arrive, we let nature take its course."

Mennas paused to let the plan sink in.

"These wallabies are a gift to us, Commander. Who cares where they came from? We have an opportunity to appease the dog pack at no cost to our mob. You can't pass that up. Be true to your mob."

The commander struggled with the ruthlessness of the idea, but his responsibility was with his mob, not to the three strangers. If sacrificing them would keep the dogs at bay, it might buy the joeys some time and give them a chance to establish themselves as adults. Though the plan was evil, it might save some of his mob, and it seemed he had little choice.

"All right."

"You've made a wise decision, Commander." Mennas' words slithered through his teeth, binding the two in darkness. Evil loves a friend.

"Rather ironic, don't you think, that the reason they approached us was to find safety in a mob?"

"Yes, rather," replied Mennas, wringing his paws as a sinister grin creased his face.

"Put four guards up at the rock pit to make sure our visitors don't leave. And needless to say, tell no one of our plan. The others may not like it or, worse, might get the idea that they're next."

He paused.

"We'll send Doogan up tomorrow night to get the job done."

DISENCHANTED

The secret to happiness is freedom.

And the secret to freedom is courage.

- Thucydides

Wally woke before dawn on the cold stone bed, the events of the previous day still turning in his mind. The mob, the commander, Jake and Peg, what he should do, it was all just a mess of confusion. And besides all that, he was sure his knee had improved, so he was disappointed it had been so easily noticed. After letting the thoughts ruffle his mood, he decided to get up and stretch his legs. A good hop might clear his mind and loosen some of the bruises from the trip down the river.

Jake and Peg were still fast asleep, but he could see Darcy was awake, his bright eyes shining in the darkness.

"Darcy," he whispered.

"What?"

"I'm going out for a hop. Can you let Jake and Peg know when they wake up? I'll be back later today."

"It's a bit dark for that, isn't it?" Darcy asked. "And should you really be going off on your own?"

"I'll be fine," Wally assured him. "Just tell Jake and Peg, okay?"

"Okay, no worries," said Darcy, unsure if he'd be awake by the time Peg and Jake woke up. Especially Jake.

Wally made his way up through the entrance to the rock pit and noticed four large wallabies sleeping just past the edge.

"I wonder what those wallabies are doing so far from the rest of the mob. If I didn't know better, I'd think they were guarding us," he thought, then dismissed the idea as nonsense. After all, why would they need to be guarded if they'd chosen to be there?

He followed the trail back down through the rocks, past the sleeping mob, just as the light of day started to signal the dawn. He paused to scan the landscape and decided to head to the river and start the day with a cool drink.

By the time he reached the river, the sun was already painting colours on the land. He dipped his nose and lapped at the water eagerly. As he watched the water flowing by, he imagined himself back in the current, carried helplessly downstream, careering through the rapids. A shiver ran down his back and he shook his head. He had been lucky to survive, and it would be a long time before he ventured back into a river like that again.

He gazed across the water to a tree that resembled the one the three of them had rested under when they first arrived at the river. He couldn't be sure if it was the same tree, but he could remember the joy of the moment. 'Clean and clear, like it's just fallen from the sky.' They had realised the dream that they had hatched on that first day of the journey, but Wally was beginning to understand that there was more to the dream than just food and water.

To have come so far, only to find a mob that was so reluctant to take them in, was unsettling. They were all wallabies, why was the commander making it so difficult? Wally had naively thought they'd be welcomed, praised even, for crossing such a barren land, and even more so, having conquered the Divide. But it seemed the achievement was completely lost on the mob, like they didn't believe it had happened at all. Part of him hated the thought of living among such suspicion, but he knew the mob's priority was to protect itself. And he knew Jake and Peg would probably be happy to stay.

He chewed on the soft grass by the side of the river, mulling the thoughts over. Eventually, his mind wandered to Gus. He'd seemed content living on his own. But would he be there if he had found another mob of Parmas? Probably not. The more Wally thought about it, the more dejected he became.

To shake his darkening mood, he turned and took off, slowly at first and then gathering pace, until the wind was whistling in his ears. The feeling of being in full flight brought a smile to his face as his mind focused on his movement rather than his troubles.

Before long, he found himself high on a hill, breathless and alone. Rocky Hill was a long way in the distance and he could even trace the river from the hill to the waterfall.

"It's still a beautiful place, regardless of what's happened," he thought, and slowly a feeling of pride started to return. He had done an incredible thing, all three of them had, best not forget that.

Thirsty again after the long hop, he headed back down toward the river. He realised he was not that far from the waterfall; maybe he could stop by and see if Gus was awake.

After an easy hop down the hill, Wally arrived at the rock platform by the waterfall. He approached the edge cautiously and looked out at the rock that had saved his life. It had been a close call, only two good jumps separated it from the falls. He took a drink and tried to keep that thought in his mind as he made his way up the hill to Gus's den.

"Gus?" he called softly as he approached, "Are you there?"

"I'm here," said Gus. "Is that you, Wally?"

"Yes," Wally replied, shuffling through the space between the rocks. "I was just out for a hop, giving my knee some exercise, and thought I'd drop by. Hope I'm not intruding."

"Not at all," said Gus warmly. "Come in, come in. I wasn't expecting to see you so soon. Did you find the mob you were looking for?"

"Yes, we did," Wally said, looking away.

Gus picked up on Wally's tone immediately. "Was it not what you were expecting?"

"Well, it certainly wasn't a friendly welcome," Wally replied. "It was almost as though they didn't want us in their mob. They called us sickly and didn't believe that we'd come through the Divide. In the end, they said we could join, but we can't live amongst the mob until we've proven we're not carrying any disease."

"Good heavens," said Gus. "That doesn't sound right. Anyone can see you're not sick. A little skinny, maybe, but not sick. That doesn't sound right at all."

"They live on a rocky hill and they have us staying in a rock pit on one side. There's barely any grass on that side, so we have to leave to eat. But it's a start, I suppose. We'll fatten up in a couple of weeks, maybe they'll be more accepting of us then."

"Maybe," said Gus, considering the situation. "But is that how you'd treat three strangers looking for a mob?"

"Of course not. I would have invited them in and introduced them to the mob at the very least. I'm pretty disappointed by the way we've been treated, but then I'm not a mob commander, and it wouldn't be the first time I've disagreed with one."

"I don't blame you. I'd be disappointed too."

"Especially after everything we went through to get here."

"Well, you seem to have done all right without a mob so far. What makes you think you need one now?"

"Protection," said Wally, like the answer was tattooed on his tongue. "More eyes watching out for you."

"Oh, that old line," said Gus. "You think it's better to rely on others for your safety."

"Well, yes," Wally said. "You must know it's safer in a mob than alone."

"Is it?" Gus asked.

"Of course it is. Every wallaby knows that."

"I suppose there was a time when I would have agreed with you, but I haven't been in a mob for a long time now. I'm surviving pretty well without one. Seems to me the idea of mob 'protection' relies on trusting others to look after you. Why would you need that if you can look after yourself?"

Gus paused, but he wasn't really looking for an answer. "To be honest, the whole idea seems dangerous to me. The more you rely on others, the lazier you get. It's that laziness that dulls the very senses you need."

Wally had never heard anyone speak that way about the wallaby code, and he couldn't really fault Gus's logic.

"To a predator," Gus continued, "a mob must look like an all-you-can-eat buffet, there are plenty of choices. If I were a predator, it would make more sense to go after a large mob than a couple of strays in the open field, don't you think? Especially if the entire mob was gathered on one rocky hill."

"I suppose," said Wally, thinking about Gus's words.

"But mob life is the wallaby way. You don't abandon your mob. The ones who go off on their own get taken."

As soon as the words were out of his mouth, Wally realised what he had said. Gus looked at him in disbelief.

"Really? Did the three of you get taken?"

"Well, we came close," Wally said, trying to

justify his statement, knowing it was far too late for that.

"And here I am. I'm not 'taken' either. So that's four out of four of us who have left their mob and survived. Have you ever seen the carcass of a wallaby that left their mob?"

"No."

"And what do you think your old mob is saying about the three of you now? That you left and went on to find a land where food and water is plentiful? That you were able to survive on your wits alone? That you didn't need the mob?"

"No. They are probably saying we were taken by dingoes before we were even out of earshot." Wally heard the echo of Jake's words from the day before they left their mob.

"Most likely. A mob has to believe in the mob. Otherwise, there is no point to it, and it disintegrates."

"Are you suggesting we shouldn't have joined that mob?"

"I'm just saying you should believe in yourself at least as much as you believe in a mob. Make sure there's a real reason for being there. I know what you're feeling. It feels good to be a part of something bigger than yourself, something that wraps itself around you like a blanket on a cold night, but nothing will take care of you better than yourself."

Wally thought about what Gus was saying. It was against everything that he'd ever been taught. Were they just being lazy? Just looking for something bigger to look after them? Passing on the responsibility to someone else?

"I've never heard anyone say that out loud before."

"I'll bet you haven't. I hope you'll excuse me for saying this, but I got the impression that you didn't really want to join that mob in the first place. That day when your friends arrived, after you were nearly washed over the falls. It seemed to me like you were going to find that mob because that's what your friends wanted. You didn't really want to join that mob at all, did you?"

"No."

The honesty of the answer surprised even Wally.

"I would have been just as happy to keep going."

"Sounds like the three of you may have had slightly different intentions from the start."

"I guess so," Wally replied. "When we left, I just wanted to find a better place to live, and I was tired of our old commander's reluctance to do anything about our lack of food and water. Finding another mob hadn't even occurred to me until we saw those wallabies at the river and Jake and Peg seemed so intent on finding them. I can understand what they wanted, but I felt like I was losing my independence, that I would just become another small face in a big crowd."

"That you would lose some of the responsibility for yourself and your friends? That you were losing control, perhaps?"

"Yes, that too, but I could also see the benefits. The safety, the community, and most of all it seemed to be what Jake and Peg wanted. They're my best friends, I didn't want to lose them, so how could I deny them that?"

"Well, you lost something in that decision."

"What do you mean by that?" Wally asked.

"You decided to stay with your friends. That was to your benefit, but it cost you what you wanted, which was to keep the adventure going."

The haze began to clear in Wally's mind. The way Gus explained it made it seem so simple.

"I doubt you'll be happy in that mob," continued Gus. "You just don't seem convinced that it's right for you. I think you'll need to revisit that decision or adjust your priorities."

"I'm starting to think I won't be happy either way. You're saying leave my friends and keep my freedom, or keep my friends and lose my freedom."

"I didn't say it was an easy choice or even the only one. Maybe the mob will turn out to be better than you think. If you leave, maybe your friends will decide to leave with you. Maybe it is time for you to settle down, and you just need to get used to the idea of a new mob. Maybe you just need to give it some time."

"Time," Wally repeated, irritated by the suggestion. "I probably should have seen this coming. I was naïve to think our journey would go on forever. I suppose it was always going to come to this, I just wasn't ready to face the moment. Or more honestly, I didn't want to."

The air was getting heavy with the weight of the discussion. Wally seemed lost in his thoughts, so Gus thought it would be best to change the subject.

"Well, I'm sure you'll figure it out, one way or another. Now how about a game of Jogi? It's been quite a while since I've had a real opponent. Needles and Pins don't really understand it."

"Okay," Wally said. It had been a long time since he'd played the game too. He used to be good at it, he hoped he still was, and maybe it would take his mind off the mob.

Gus drew up a board in the dirt and collected the stones, handing Wally his share. They carefully placed their stones on the board, and Gus invited Wally to make the first move. The conversation faded as they focused on the game. Move by move, the game progressed, as each wallaby tried to understand the other's strategy and gain the upper hand. Finally, Gus broke the silence.

"How long has it been since you've played?"

"I think the last time I played I was barely older than a joey. Life was a lot less complicated then."

"You mean you were a lot less complicated, don't you?" Gus captured two of Wally's stones. "I doubt life has changed much."

"Well, let's just say I was a lot happier then."

Wally thought back to the time when he was a joey, when every journey seemed like an adventure and every little thing was a discovery. Learning to hop, racing the other joeys, looking up into night skies filled with a million stars and feeling the soothing touch of rain on his fur. Despite the trouble he had with his knee, he had enjoyed his childhood, free as it was, of responsibilities and care.

He countered Gus's move with a block.

"Well, nothing's changed except you." Gus jumped one of Wally's stones, slid across, jumped another, slid across and jumped another, collecting three more of Wally's pebbles. "Happiness is within you, Wally, right where you left it when you were a joey."

Stung by the loss of three stones, Wally reacted without thinking and immediately took one of Gus's stones.

"Don't confuse happiness with the way you've decided to look at things," Gus said, as he took advantage of Wally's move by taking two more of his stones.

"I'm not sure how I could look at things differently. I really thought we'd made it when we came through the Divide, that most of my troubles were behind me. But it seems all I've done is find a new set of problems. The mob, Jake and Peg, it's not turning out as I hoped it would."

"Maybe you only read the first page of the map," said Gus. "But at least you're looking at one. Maybe you just need to look a little further down the track."

"What are you suggesting I do?"

"Do you want to stay in that mob?"

"No."

"Then move on."

"And turn my back on Jake and Peg?"

"I don't think you'll last in that mob, so if your friends decide to stay, leaving them is only a matter of time. Everyone has a path, Wally. Follow yours or you'll never be happy. And bear in mind, if you do decide to leave the mob, your friends will have a decision of their own to make. Look inside. I'm only telling you what you already know."

"You want me to become like you, a wallaby without a mob?"

He took another of Gus' stones.

"Believe me, Wally, if I could find a Parma

mob, I'd join it. You're not in the same boat. There are plenty of mobs of your kind, you don't have to settle in the first one you find. Life is a bit like Jogi. You need to see every move to the end, otherwise you just end up hoping for the best, and we both know how that usually turns out. If you're still unsure, just ask yourself, 'Where will this path lead me?'. Follow through until you can see the answer as clearly as you can, and if you don't like it, don't go down that path. Where do you think you'll end up if you join that mob?"

Wally thought about the mob, how he would feel living under the commander's law and the influence of the crooked-looking wallaby that sat at the commander's right hand. Having to prove himself to be treated as anything more than an outcast. While the picture painted itself in his mind, Gus made one final move and trapped Wally's last pebble. The game was over.

"You thrashed me," admitted Wally as he looked down at the board.

"I think your mind may have been on more than just the game."

Wally looked down at his last pathetic pebble, now captured, and suddenly felt just like it, a tiny stone in a much bigger game.

"I don't think I was much of an opponent. How about another game?" Wally asked.

"Excellent," replied Gus, as he shared out the stones and the two began setting up the board again.

Wally began to reflect on what life would be like if he decided to leave. He remembered the last time he was on his own, when he left Jake and Peg at Dot's while he went ahead. He remembered the loneliness, the vulnerability, and he remembered the thrill of absolute freedom and the wonder of the unknown. Gus's argument flew in the face of everything he had been taught, but how could he have been taught anything else? It was the doctrine of a mob he was born into. 'Everyone has a path', Gus had said, and Wally was finding it harder and harder to believe that his path led to the Rocky Hill mob. But if he did leave, where did his path lead? Which way would he go?

"Gus," he said as he placed his last stone on the board, "when you decided to go looking for another mob, what made you come this way? You said you were from the north, why did you come south?"

"I didn't. I did what you did. I went east, into the sun. Then I got to the ocean and had to come back inland."

"The ocean?"

"Have you never seen the ocean?"

"I don't think so. What is it?"

"Oh, Wally, you'd know if you'd seen it!" said Gus. "It's the most water you'll ever see, it makes that river look like a trickle. It's so big you can't see the other side, and it sparkles in the sunshine.

Waves of water roll onto soft sand at the edges and lull you to sleep at night. Sometimes it's so violent that the water seems to erupt off the cliffs; at other times it's as gentle as a still lake. And at night, under a full moon, well, it's impossible to describe the beauty of it."

The memory silenced Gus for a moment before he went on.

"You have to see it for yourself, Wally, to understand it, to understand how it connects everything. If you're looking for a new direction, that's the place I'd go."

"How would I find it?"

"Just follow the river, it will take you there."

The ember of adventure suddenly blazed in Wally's mind. For Wally, it was like another piece of a puzzle had fallen into place.

The Jogi continued well into the afternoon, and the games became more entertaining as Wally's attention was directed on his play, seeing each move to the end. By late afternoon, Gus had won three games and Wally two, although Wally insisted that the first game didn't count.

"Every move counts," was all Gus had to say about that.

As the shadows grew longer and the sun sank lower in the sky, Wally suddenly realised that the day was almost gone.

"It's getting late, Gus. I'd better get back to

Jake and Peg, they're probably starting to worry about me," he said, helping Gus pick up the pebbles from the last match. "I've really enjoyed today. I'm glad I stopped by."

"I'm glad too," said Gus. "I've enjoyed having another wallaby to talk to. Try as I might, I just can't get interested in Needles' and Pins' ants. Drop by anytime, and if you do decide to leave, make sure you stop in to say goodbye."

"Thanks, Gus, I will," he promised. He turned and said goodbye to the echidnas, then made his way out of the den.

"See you, Gus."

"Safe trip!" Gus called after him.

He walked down to the river and looked out once more at the rock that had saved his life. He remembered his thoughts on the rock, seeing Jake and Peg on the far side, wondering if they would come looking for him or whether their ways had finally parted.

But they had come, and they had found him.

He took a long drink, then turned for the journey back to the mob, the thoughts of the day swimming in his head.

"Look inside," he thought.

And within moments the confusion disappeared, and he knew exactly what he had to do.

ALL FOR THREE

By the time Wally returned to the mob, dusk was falling. Though he had made his decision, every step closer to Jake and Peg deepened his apprehension about what he was about to tell them. He kept trying to think of a way to break the news to them, but he knew there was no better way than just telling them straight out. The thought turned his stomach.

He followed the path into the rocky hillside, heading up toward the rock pit, knowing this would be the last time he would return to the Rocky Hill mob. His mind spun a thousand silent stories of what would happen to him after that night, alone again in the wilderness. But despite his dread about telling Jake and Peg, he knew, for him, leaving was the right thing to do.

As he approached the pit, he was surprised to see the same four wallabies, almost blocking the path.

"G'day," he said cautiously as he passed. The wallabies watched him pass in silence, and as soon as he was clear of them, one of them raced back down the hill.

"Strange," thought Wally as he continued along the path.

When he finally reached the rock pit, he stood at the rim to find Jake and Peg lying in the centre.

Peg glanced up and immediately got to her feet. "Finally, Wally! Where have you been?"

"I just went out for a hop and ended up at Gus's," he replied as he hopped down into the pit. "Didn't Darcy tell you? I left early this morning and didn't want to wake you. Is something wrong?"

"Yes, there's something wrong! When Jake and I woke up, we went out to find something to eat and drink. Everywhere we went, we were followed by those four goons sitting just past the entrance to the pit. They wouldn't let us go beyond this side of the hill, and we can't move without being shadowed. We had no idea where you were. Darcy's been asleep all day. Didn't you get followed?"

"No," said Wally. "Like I said, I left early."

"Well, it's like we're being watched or guarded or something. The welcome was bad enough, but keeping us in this stupid pit and the constant shadowing? I just don't get it, Wally. Something's not right."

"Is it really such a big deal, Peg?" Jake asked. "So they're keeping an eye on us. So what? We know they don't want us mixing with the mob."

"They're watching *everything*, Jake," Peg insisted. "I don't like it. That doesn't happen in any mob I've ever heard of. It's wrong, and it's not what I expected when we came here. I'm telling you, something's going on, and I want out."

"Out?" Wally asked. "You mean out of the mob?"

"Yes, out of the mob. I don't deserve to be treated like this. We haven't done anything wrong, and I won't be a part of a mob that treats me like an outcast." The more Peg spoke, the more resolute she became. "This was a mistake. I'm sure we can find a better mob further down the track."

"Funny you should say that," said Wally, relieved he wouldn't be leaving alone. "I wasn't planning to stay either. Jake?"

"Seriously? We just got here!" Jake moaned. "Oh, whatever! I don't like this place any more than you two do. Okay, all for three and one for three or whatever that saying is."

"All for one and one for all," Wally corrected, the words dripping with the guilt of having decided to leave his friends if it came to that. "All right, it's settled then. We leave first thing in the morning," he said, looking over to Peg.

All he received was a determined nod.

As the twilight turned to darkness, the three

wallabies settled, their restless minds a terrible concoction of disappointment, relief, and righteousness. Wally hoped there wouldn't be any trouble when they left. He didn't want another clash with the commander. He resolved to wake before dawn so they could leave early, before the rest of the mob was awake.

Gradually, they fell asleep, knowing it would be a big day tomorrow, just as Darcy began to stir. He wriggled out of Peg's pouch to find the three wallabies already fast asleep.

"Jake. Peg," he whispered. "Wally's gone for a hop. Oh, never mind."

He scampered across the rock pit and slipped into the night, his big eyes already adjusted to the dark. At the top of the pit, he saw he could reach the tree on the top of the hill, and from there he could glide down into the lush treetops that sheltered the mob. It wouldn't take long. He was sure he'd be back before anyone noticed.

He raced across the stones to the tree and climbed quickly up its trunk.

"Flying again!" he thought, a smile beaming across his face, as he launched himself into the night.

Down, down, down he soared, the slightest twitch in his legs guiding him through the air toward a gum tree humming with insects. He lifted his arms and landed gracefully on the trunk.

Pausing to get his bearings, he heard the faint

sound of voices nearby. He crept along a branch and peered over the edge to see the commander and Mennas talking, as Doogan came to join them.

"Evening, Doogan. Thanks for coming at such short notice," said the commander casually. "I have an important job for you."

Doogan said nothing. Being called up to see the commander meant he wanted something done, and it wouldn't be pleasant.

"The dogs will be here tomorrow. I trust you know what that means."

Doogan nodded. They all knew what that meant.

"Good. It seems the three wallabies who joined us recently are carrying a serious disease. One that could endanger the entire mob." He moved deliberately around the small den. "Your mob," he said, catching Doogan's eye. "We can't allow them to put us all at risk. I'm sure you understand that."

Doogan stared at the commander, silent.

"Unfortunately, those three will soon succumb to their illness and perish, so I intend to use them to appease the dogs, to save the members of our own mob."

Doogan knew the commander was lying. He knew there was nothing wrong with the three wallabies that a few good lunches wouldn't fix. But he knew when to keep his mouth shut. He hadn't risen to the commander's side by questioning his authority.

"What do you want me to do?"

"You must see to it that the three wallabies are no longer able to jump. That way, when the dogs attack, they will go for them instead of the mob. Even though they're skinny, they should be enough to satisfy the pack, and while the dogs are occupied, the mob will have a chance to escape. Go to the rock pit while they're asleep and disable them. Do you understand?"

Doogan looked at the commander, struggling to believe what the commander had just asked him to do.

"You want me to break their legs?"

"It's for the good of the mob, Doogan. Sacrificing those three doomed wallabies will save many more of our own. Take someone you trust and be as quick as you can, then get out of there. No one else can know about this. Understood?"

Doogan nodded slowly. He had done some awful things for the commander, but this was by far the worst. He would be ensuring the death of three of his own kind. The request struck a sickening chord in him as his eyes locked with the commander's. When would enough become too much?

"Do it for your mob, Doogan, for the joeys," pressed the commander, sensing his resistance. "I know I can rely on you. I trust you above all."

Rather than encourage Doogan, the words only served to hollow him out. Doogan nodded, then turned and left the commander and Mennas to their scheming.

"Curse those dogs and their grisly raids," he thought.

Darcy couldn't believe what he'd just heard. He had to get back and warn Wally, Jake, and Peg!

He scurried along the limb and leapt into the night, sailing through the darkness until he touched down on a gum tree that grew out of the side of the hill. He quickly climbed up to another branch, his mind working quickly to plot his course through the trees back to the three wallabies.

"That tree could lead to that tree, then that one," he thought, quickly putting the flight path together. "From there it's just a short run home." He tensed his legs to jump, but before he could leap, he felt a large, clawed foot come down squarely across his back.

"Hello, little mouse," croaked the owl.

THE OWL

Darcy had been so worried about getting back to the wallabies that he hadn't seen the owl hiding in the shadows.

"Thinking of flying over to that gum tree, were you? That's a long flight for a little mouse like you, isn't it?"

"Sugar glider," protested Darcy, the pressure on his back making it difficult to speak. "I'm not a mouse, I'm a sugar glider. And for your information, I could make that flight easily."

The owl let out a ghastly cackle. "Oh really?" she croaked. "Quite the little pilot, are you? Well, how about you and I have some fun. I'll show you what flying is all about. Go on then, glide over to that tree and let's see how far you get. If you can make it, you're free to go." She began to lift her foot from Darcy's back. "But I'll have you back before you're halfway there."

As soon as Darcy felt the pressure lift, he jumped. He flew off into the night, zigzagging through the air. He tried every trick he knew to evade the owl, but his little flaps of skin were no match for her wings. The owl swooped down and caught him easily in mid-air.

"That was too easy, my little mouse! It was almost like you were floating in mid-air! You'll have to do better than that. How about you have another try?"

The owl flew back to an even higher branch and set Darcy down.

"Come on, little mouse. Don't be frightened. You can have your freedom if you can outfly me," she said. "But try to make it interesting this time, will you? Give me a challenge!"

She watched Darcy's every move. He glared at her, then looked out over the trees and suddenly threw himself off the branch. He curled up into a tight ball and dropped into a terrifying free fall.

The owl rolled her eyes and barely moved.

Faster and faster Darcy plummeted toward the earth. "Not yet," he thought, "not yet."

The ground raced up at him, and at the very last moment he threw out his arms and legs like a parachute to cushion the impact.

The owl had seen through the plan and timed her interception perfectly. She snatched Darcy out of the air just as his limbs extended.

With almost no effort at all, she flew back up into the tree and set Darcy down again.

"Did you really think that would work? You have no idea, do you, little mouse? I am a master of flight. The best you can do is glide. I'm getting bored with our game already."

Darcy knew she was right. He was no match for the owl in the air, and if he didn't think of something quickly, it was only a matter of time before the game would come to a gruesome end. Worse still, if he didn't get back to Wally and warn him about the commander's plan, it would be all over for the wallabies too.

He looked back up at the owl as his own words spoke to him. 'He was no match for the owl in the air...'

"Yak, yak, yak, owl. You're pretty full of yourself, aren't you? Anyone would think you were the greatest flyer the world had ever seen. If you think you're so good, why don't we make it interesting? Why don't you turn away next time, so you're not watching which way I jump?"

"Ha!" scoffed the owl. "That won't make any difference. I can see the slightest movement in the darkest places. I'll spot you in a flash and be on you before you can think."

"Yak, yak, yak."

"You cheeky little squeak!"

The owl grabbed Darcy, flew out to the end of the branch and set him down.

"All right," she said. "I'll turn around, and you

do your best, but this time I'll be catching you with my beak."

"Fine," said Darcy bravely, though he felt anything but brave inside.

He watched as the owl's head rotated on her body so that, while her body still faced him, her eyes did not. Darcy didn't move. Sensing no motion, the owl grew suspicious and snapped her head back around.

"Hold on!" complained Darcy. "I haven't decided which way I'm going yet! You're cheating! Are you scared you'll lose, owl?"

"Don't taunt me, little mouse, or I'll end this now. Now hurry up and make up your mind." The owl slowly turned her head all the way around again.

This time, Darcy didn't wait. As soon as the owl's head was turned, he ran straight under the branch and held on tight.

The owl heard the movement and whipped her head around, but there was no sign of Darcy. Not in the air, not on the ground. It was as though he'd vanished!

The owl hopped over to where Darcy had been standing and stooped over to get a better look. From under the branch, Darcy watched as her sharp black claws sunk into the bark. As she leaned further over, Darcy raced up behind her and, in a split second, had jumped onto her back, digging his claws into the thin skin on the back of her head.

The owl shrieked in pain as Darcy latched on.

He leaned forward and looked straight into the owl's enormous eyes. "Now you listen to me, you miserable bird. You're going to fly me back to my friends or I'll rip every feather off your ugly head. Starting with this one!" Darcy grabbed a feather and yanked it out.

"Raaaarrrrkkkk! You're hurting me!" screeched the owl.

"Just fly!" shouted Darcy as he ripped out another long feather.

The owl leapt into the night air with Darcy hanging for dear life, steering the owl by pulling the feathers on her head in the direction he needed to go.

"Woohoo!" Darcy cried. "You're right, owl! This is what I call flying!"

The wind flattened his ears as they flew through the air at what seemed like impossible speed. Turning and twisting through branches, sweeping upwards at the slightest movement of a wing, he flew the owl higher and higher, circling above the mob until the rock pit came into view. He pushed her into a sweeping dive, marvelling at the effortless agility of her silent wings as she carried him back to the wallabies.

As they neared the pit, Darcy pushed her head lower and lower until they were barely skimming above the ground.

Closer, closer, nearly there...

"And here's something to take home with you!" he shouted as he leapt from her back, taking another handful of feathers with him.

He spread his limbs to soften the landing but misjudged his speed and crashed into Jake's belly with a loud thump.

Jake was up in a flash. "What the devil was that?"

"Sorry, Jake, it's just me. Darcy. That was amazing!" he cried, lost for a moment in the thrill of the flight and the clutch of feathers in his tiny hand. Then he remembered the commander's plan. "Hey, you three have to get out of here. That big wallaby is coming to break your legs!" He looked up to see a nearly bald owl flying away.

"What?" Jake asked. "What are you talking about?"

Darcy quickly told Jake the whole story, how he had glided down to the trees above the mob, overheard the commander's conversation with Mennas and Doogan, and how the big wallaby was probably already on his way up to carry out the commander's diabolical plan.

Jake woke Peg and Wally immediately.

"Are you sure that's what they said?" asked Peg after hearing the story from Darcy. "How could they even think of doing that? To their own kind! What kind of monsters are they?"

"Well, there's no sense waiting around to find out. Let's just get out of here," said Wally.

But as he turned to leave, he looked up to see the imposing silhouette of Doogan and another large wallaby, blocking the entrance to the pit.

A PLAN

Shar came to collect Caper the next morning and waited until the dingo began to stir.

"Hello, Chief. I trust you slept well last night?"

"Yes," replied Caper groggily.

"That's good, because today is the day we hunt the wallabies."

Suddenly, Caper was alert and on his feet. He had rested well, and yesterday's turkey had returned the strength to his limbs and finally silenced his belly. Now it was back to the job at hand, finding those wallabies.

"So, tell me about the three wallabies you saw," Caper said.

"Well, two of them came down the far side of the river. The other must have been swept in, as he was already in the water by the time he arrived at the waterfall. Heaven knows how he didn't drown, but he flipped himself up onto a rock at the top of the waterfall. The other two tried to find a way across, but that was a waste of time; the river is far too treacherous when it's this high, so they made their way down to the bank below the waterfall. The one on the rock must have jumped ashore at some point because he was no longer there the next time I looked."

"I know the one," Caper seethed. "He's the one that led us up the ramp. The one that caused Knuth to jump."

"Was Knuth a friend of yours?"

"He was our leader. He died chasing that lousy wallaby."

"How awful," said Shar, feigning sympathy.

"What happened then?" asked Caper.

"The two wallabies on the other side of the river did what you did. They crossed the river by walking behind the waterfall. I had no idea you could do that! It must have been exciting, jumping through that wall of water."

"Not really," said Caper, remembering his struggle in the turbulence of the waterfall. "What happened to the wallaby that was on the rock?"

"I've got no idea. I watched the other two cross before I went to check on him, but by the time I got there, he was gone."

"Why didn't you just go and wait on the bank for him?" asked Caper.

"I would have lost sight of the other two if I'd done that, and I wanted to see what all three were doing. I misjudged the one on the rock. He was pretty banged up; I thought he would be there longer than he was."

"Did you see where the other two went, once they'd crossed?"

"The other two came up the bank next to the waterfall. There's a trail down to the bottom of the falls on this side. Then all three met up where the first one jumped ashore. They're resting not far from there, just a little way up the hill."

"Why haven't you attacked them?"

"I can't take on three wallabies by myself! I'm just not big enough. I need someone like you, strong, ferocious and clever. We make a good team, Caper. Catching a wallaby together should be child's play."

"Yes, child's play," said Caper, his eyes narrowing at the thought of the attack. The flattery slid into his ears like oil into a rusty wheel. His ego had taken quite a battering at the hands of the wallabies, and it was good to finally have someone on his side.

"I'm not interested in any other wallabies right now. I just want those three."

Everything the fox had said matched the evidence Caper had gathered: the three sets of tracks turning into two, the hurried chase of the pair of tracks along the river, the confusion at the top of the waterfall and again at the base of the waterfall, the sighting of the wallaby on the rock, and even the crossing behind the waterfall. The fox seemed to have witnessed it all. And now, with any luck, he would lead Caper straight to their hiding place.

"Well then," said Shar, "we might as well get moving. It's a long way back to the waterfall from here. We'll be lucky to get there before late afternoon."

Shar led Caper through the bush and soon realised that the dingo was nowhere near as agile as he was. Caper was too big to squeeze through the gaps in the undergrowth that posed no problem for the fox. His clumsy movements frustrated them both, and he was slowing them down. "Perhaps we should go the easy way," Shar thought. "That dingo will take forever this way."

"Not much further," he said. "Then the going gets easier."

"About time!" said Caper. "This isn't even a track!"

They finally reached a small trail that led them through the hills. It was a longer way around, but they began to make good progress. Even so, it wasn't until late afternoon that they finally arrived in the hills above the waterfall.

"There it is," said Shar, as the waterfall came into view. "At last."

It had been a full day's walk with the clumsy dingo, and the fox was tired.

"Okay," Caper said darkly, "let's go find those wallabies."

"Now?" Shar asked with surprise. "Caper, I think it would be foolish to go now. We should go in the morning when we are fresh and surprise them. They won't be expecting us then, and they won't stand a chance. It's almost dark; if we go now, we may not get all of them."

Caper could see the logic in the fox's advice but struggled with the patience to wait another day.

"What do we do until then?"

"How about we find another turkey?" asked the fox, smiling, his plan finally falling into place.

TRAPPED

"Darcy, hop in," said Peg as she looked up at the two big wallabies. She silently kicked herself for not listening to her instincts. Why hadn't she? They had been right every single time. Deep down, she knew why. Her desire to find a place to settle down, a new mob and new friends, had been far too strong for her inner voice. And now that voice was speaking to her again in an 'I-told-you-so' kind of way: "Here we go again."

Darcy jumped into her pouch, and she readied herself for the confrontation.

Jake was the one to break the silence.

"G'day. What are you two doing up so late? It's a bit unusual to be hopping around at this time of night, isn't it?"

"I could ask you the same question," replied Doogan.

"Well, it's not easy to sleep on these rocks. In fact, we haven't slept much at all since we got here. But I guess you'd know that, wouldn't you? You haven't let us out of your sight, following us around, watching our every move. If you don't mind me saying, you haven't exactly been the best of hosts. But fortunately for us, here's your chance to redeem yourself. We were just leaving, so maybe you two can give us an escort out of here, you know, in case there are any wild dogs in the area."

"You're not going anywhere," said Doogan, without flinching.

Wally desperately tried to think of a way out of the pit while Jake held their attention, but there was only one way out, and that was through Doogan and his stooge.

"And why is that?" Jake asked, leading them on.

"You know why. I heard the three of you talking just now with that little sugar glider."

"Oh, you mean the part about you coming here to break our legs so that you can sacrifice us to a pack of dogs? To be frank, that doesn't sound too appealing. In fact, it sounds downright unpleasant. I mean, what on earth is wrong with you? You don't have to give up your own just to keep the dogs happy. You're not even trying to evade them. You've grown weak. Weak-willed and weak-spirited. So I've got some bad news for you. We'll be long gone before the dogs arrive."

Wally turned to Peg and said quietly, "There's only one way out of here, Peg, and it's pretty much the same as in the clearing. Except this time, we're just going to have to charge at them. They've got the advantage of the high ground, but we've got the numbers. When we go, give it everything you've got until we're out of this pit."

"I'll make this easier for you," said Doogan. "We only need two of you to keep the dogs happy. One of you can go."

"You're all heart," Jake shot back. "But we don't work that way. We look after each other. Besides, why would we trust you? Just come on in and get us. We'll sort this out right now."

"Don't move," Doogan said to the other wallaby.

Jake turned to Wally and Peg and said quietly, "Are you two ready?"

"Yep," said Wally, resigned to the fact that there was going to be a fight.

"You know there's only one way out of here, right?" asked Jake.

Wally nodded. "Focus all our force on the largest obstruction."

"I was going to say 'Smash into Doogan as hard as we can', but I like what you said better," admitted Jake. "Once we've hit him, you take the little guy. I'll deal with Doogan. Peg, if you see an opening, take it and get out of here."

"Don't you worry about me," Peg replied, angered that Jake thought she would even consider taking off without them.

"Come on, you big sook, come and get us!" called Jake, trying to taunt Doogan as the three wallabies moved as far back in the pit as they could to maximise their run-up.

As expected, Doogan didn't move.

"Okay," said Jake. "On three."

"One..."

"Two..."

"Three!"

The wallabies charged through the pit side by side, all aiming for the main target. Jake aimed low and launched himself into the belly of Doogan; Wally came in from the side and drove his shoulder into Doogan's ribs; while Peg went high and drove a shoulder into Doogan's head. All four wallabies went down in an explosion of force, Wally to the side, Peg ended up well past Doogan, and Jake bounced backwards onto the lip of the pit.

The smaller wallaby went straight for Wally, but Wally saw him coming. He braced himself on the ground, lined up the attacker, and unleashed a ferocious kick to the other wallaby's belly. A searing pain shot through Wally's knee as the joint twisted with the force of the blow. He cried out as the other wallaby stumbled and fell backwards down the hill.

Peg was through the blockade and free to run, but when she looked back, she saw Doogan already advancing on Jake, while Wally struggled to get to his feet.

Jake scrambled to clear the edge of the pit but couldn't move quickly enough to regain his footing. The huge wallaby was almost upon him.

"Looks like you'll be the first for the dogs," Doogan said as he prepared to land a crippling blow.

There was nothing Jake could do. Lying on his back, he braced for the big wallaby's kick. But as Doogan moved forward, Peg charged.

"Not likely!" she cried as she went airborne, twisting sideways in mid-flight. She landed the full force of both her hind legs to the back of Doogan's head.

Doogan lurched forward as Jake rolled toward him, tripping him. His balance lost, Doogan tipped forward, over the edge and down into the bowels of the pit.

"Come on!" Wally cried. "Let's go!"

All three were quickly on their feet, bounding down the path, when they heard Doogan raise the alarm.

"Stop them!"

As Wally came charging down the hill, he could see the four guards already blocking the path ahead. Despite the terrible pain in his knee, he bounded on.

"Get out of my way!" he shouted as he charged the blockade.

The four wallabies braced themselves for impact, but none were expecting what happened next.

Wally was accelerating fast when his wobbly knee misfired, launching him into a backward somersault, right over the top of the four guards.

The guards were astonished by the manoeuvre.

"Did you see that?" one asked, as they all turned to see Wally land perfectly back on his feet.

"He does that all the time," said Peg, as she and Jake barrelled into the backs of the guards, sending them crashing down like tenpins.

The three wallabies tore down the rocky slope, finding their way in the moonlight. With one last shoulder charge to the last wallaby that stood in their way, they were back into the open and hopping madly away.

Doogan gathered himself quickly and sprinted after them, collecting the guards on the way. They chased the trio down the rocky hill and into the open field, but years of idle indulgence had diminished their endurance. The gap widened quickly, and soon, exhausted and in the dark, the Rocky Hill wallabies gave up the chase and returned to their hill.

Jake, Wally, and Peg headed across the plains

and deep into the hills beside the waterfall, where they could hide in the thick bush. When they were a good distance up the hill, Wally turned, looking for any sign of the mob wallabies.

"Looks like we've lost them."

"Good," said Jake.

"More like good riddance," said Peg. "I never want to see those lowlifes again."

"Neither do I," said Wally. "I knew something was wrong with that mob, but I wasn't expecting *that*."

"I felt that too," admitted Peg. "I should have said something."

"Well, no one could have seen that coming."

"Or your backflip," said Jake. "That knee of yours saved the day. Is it okay? We haven't seen a misfire for a while."

"I've twisted it again," replied Wally. "It's pretty painful right now, but we'll see how it is in the morning. We may have to take it easy for a while."

Approach

The next morning, Caper and Shar set out as soon as they woke. Shar had found a spot for them in the hills the night before, not far from the top of the waterfall. It was close enough that they wouldn't have far to travel in the morning, but far enough to keep Caper from jumping the gun.

Shar led Caper down to the bank where Wally had jumped ashore. The rock seemed much closer now, and Caper's gaze drifted back to the far side of the river, where he had stood just two days earlier. His confidence surged. He was finally closing in on the trio. It was only a matter of time before Knuth would be avenged.

"Here!" The fox had found Wally's footprints in the soft dirt.

Caper ran over and recognised the twisted footprint immediately. "Yes, that's him."

"They lead up this way," said Shar, pointing up the hill.

Caper followed the footprints up the trail quietly, watching for any sign of movement. His senses were on full alert now, the moment he had been waiting for was approaching.

For the first time since they had left the lake, Shar followed Caper, letting him lead the way up the path.

"There," whispered Caper. "The trail leads between those rocks."

He crept forward slowly and silently, between the two rocks that led to Gus's den, his senses tingling, the scent of wallaby thick in the air. Slowly, slowly, and the prize would soon be his.

Inside the den, Gus and the echidnas waited. Pins had spotted the fox and the dingo as soon as they arrived at the riverbank and had warned Gus. All three were now waiting in the shadows of the den, preparing for the attack.

"Steady," Gus whispered to Needles. "We want them well inside before we make our move. Are you ready, Pins?"

Pins nodded defiantly.

LEAVING

Wally woke as dawn began to break. Peg was already awake; Jake, as usual, was not.

"Can you see any wallabies from the mob?" Wally asked.

"No," replied Peg. "There hasn't been any movement. I guess they gave up searching last night. That's not to say they won't come after us in daylight, though."

"I doubt they'll be chasing us," said Wally. "They may have more to worry about than three skinny wallabies. If the dogs are on their way, they won't want to split up the mob." He paused, thinking about what he had just said. "Why do you think they called them 'dogs'? Do you think that's what they call dingoes?"

"I don't know. Maybe they're not dingoes."

Wally wondered about the dogs and why the Rocky Hill mob had become so resigned to their attacks when Jake began to stir. He cast a sleepy eye toward Wally and Peg.

"Any sign of that mob?"

"Not a peep so far," replied Wally. "They're either looking in the wrong place, or they've got something bigger to worry about."

"I still can't believe what those blokes intended to do," said Jake. "Thank heavens Darcy was there to warn us."

Darcy was still fast asleep in Peg's pouch.

"I know," said Peg. "If it wasn't for him, we'd probably still be lying in that pit." She paused for a moment and looked down at her pouch. "One thing I must ask him though, where did all these owl feathers come from?"

"Well, I'd say we're clear of that mob," said Wally. "We'd best figure out what we're going to do from here. To start with, how about we put some more distance between us and the mob and head downstream? We might as well keep the river close, there's plenty of cover on this side."

"That sounds like a plan," said Peg. "Maybe we should head to the river now and start off with a drink. I'm pretty thirsty after all that time lying in that stupid rock pit."

"All right," said Wally. "Do you two mind if we stop in at Gus's on the way? I'd like to say goodbye. We're not that far from his den, it shouldn't take us too long to get there."

"Fine with me," said Jake.

"Through here?" asked Peg, pointing toward

an opening in the bush.

"Yes, through there and down the hill," replied Wally. "We might just catch him before he takes his morning nap."

Forever

Caper paused for a moment on the narrow path. He could smell the wallaby clearly now, but it wasn't the scent of the three he had been tracking. His nose twitched, savouring the scent. It was delicious and unmistakably wallaby, but unusual, and not the smell he'd expected. And there was something else. This was a single wallaby, not three.

The fox sensed Caper's hesitation and gave him a nudge. Caper looked back, and silently, the fox signalled him to proceed.

Caper shrugged. "A wallaby is a wallaby," he thought. "If it's not the three, they'll be next." The smell of the prey drove him on as his instincts took control. He crept slowly up the path, head lowered, his senses alert.

Gus saw the dingo's nose as it came around the bend in the pathway. He was moving very slowly, deliberately. His head came into view, his dark eyes glinting in the sunlight, his lips wet for an attack.

Gus waited. "Patience," he thought. "Patience."

With each step, Caper moved closer, drawn to the prey by the magnetic scent. He inched forward, his shoulders moving into the den. He knew he was close now, peering into the shadows of the den, searching for the slightest movement that would give the prey away.

Gus braced himself with his tail, leaning back so his legs were free to kick. Needles was in position, looking back at Gus, clinging tightly to the bottom of Gus's long feet. Gus waited for his moment, as Caper's body moved slowly into the den.

"Fire!" he cried. With a mighty kick, he launched Needles straight at the unwelcome dingo.

Needles flew through the air like a cannonball, finding his mark on the dingo's left flank. His long, sharp spines pierced Caper's skin.

Caper leapt up in agony, yelping in pain as a spine twisted off Needles's back and lodged itself deep in Caper's neck.

Pins raced into position as soon as the first shot was fired.

"Fire two!" Gus shouted, and the second echidna was sent hurtling towards the dingo, scoring a direct hit to Caper's ribs. Another long spine speared into his flesh, this time between his ribs, stopping a hair's breadth from his heart.

Caper cried out again and turned to flee from the spiny attack.

Wally heard the first yelp and froze. Moments later, he heard the second yelp. There was no doubt, it was the sound of a dingo, and it was close. Immediately, he thought of his friend.

"Gus!" he cried, sprinting towards Gus's den.

The fox finally made his move. He'd been through this before and knew that once Gus had fired both shots, there would be a brief moment before he could reload. That was his chance. He tore into the den and found Gus easily. In a lightning-fast scurry, the fox had Gus by the neck in his long, sharp jaws.

Wally approached the den from above, horrified to see Gus already struggling against the fox. Without a moment's hesitation, he launched himself into the den and came down heavily on Shar's back. Shar dropped Gus as Wally's weight drove him into the dirt, breaking three of his ribs with an audible crack. Seriously injured, Shar turned and limped away, but the damage was done.

Wally rushed over to Gus, who was lying in the dirt, surrounded by Needles and Pins.

"Gus!" he cried, but he could already tell it was too late. He picked Gus up in his little paws and looked down at the wounds in his neck.

Gus looked up peacefully into Wally's eyes and managed a croaky, "Hello, Wally. Seems my time has finally come," the words struggling to escape his throat.

"Gus, you're going to be all right!" Wally insisted, tasting the lie as soon as it had left his lips.

"Listen, Wally, go to the ocean. Go east. See it for yourself," he whispered.

"Gus!"

Wally knew it was no use. Gus's wounds were fatal. As he looked down at the tiny wallaby, the shadows seemed to grow around him, almost as though they were filling the space where his life once was.

Gus's eyes began to close as Wally felt the weight of the little wallaby go limp in his arms.

"Gus!"

His tiny body sagged, his head fell back, and the very last breath of the very last Parma wallaby drifted out into the still morning air and disappeared forever.

ONE PUSH

Caper fled to the river, desperately trying to scratch the spines out of his neck and chest, but every touch sent a searing pain through his body. Blood dripped freely from the puncture wounds, and in frustration he lay down as the blood trickled down his neck.

Shar appeared soon after, having followed Caper's retreat.

Caper fired up at the sight of the fox. "You used me! You sent me in there knowing that wallaby would kick those echidnas at me. This whole ruse, this whole 'pack' thing was just a way to get you in there so you could have that wallaby for yourself, wasn't it?"

"Of course it was, you fool," winced the fox. "I've felt those spines before. And this time I was so close. So close! I had him in my jaws, I can still taste him on my lips. Then that big wallaby arrived and clobbered me! I think my ribs are broken."

"Your ribs are broken?" Caper seethed. He

rose to his feet, pain shooting through his side. His head lowered, his eyes focused, he advanced slowly on the fox. "It's going to get a lot worse than that."

"Wait, Caper, wait! I didn't mean for this to happen," Shar pleaded as he tried to evade Caper, but he could barely move his legs on the side where his ribs were broken.

Not so with Caper. Though badly injured, he was still mobile, and the fury of being played for a fool overcame his pain.

He turned on Shar and let his rage play out, all of it, the frustration and failure of the chase, the humiliation of being used, and the anger of being so badly injured for nothing. Caper didn't stop until there was little left of Shar but his thick, brown tail.

Completely exhausted from the fight and the loss of blood, Caper collapsed in the dirt, grimacing as another bolt of pain shot through him.

* * *

As Wally felt the life leave the little wallaby, he felt his own heart harden. He laid Gus down gently on the dusty floor of the den and stood up, staring down at the lifeless wallaby. By then, Peg and Jake had arrived in the den, but there was nothing they could do.

"I'll be back in a minute," said Wally, his voice

low and resolute.

"Where are you going?" asked Peg.

"I'm going to find the creature that killed Gus."

He turned away from Gus, with the vision still sharp in his mind, and followed the tracks out of the den. With every step, the hatred boiled in Wally as he thought of the animal that had taken Gus. He followed the trail of blood and pawprints down the path until he reached the scene of the fight between Caper and Shar. Clearly, something had beaten him to the fox.

His gaze shifted further along the path to the dingo, now lying motionless in the sun, two echidna spines protruding from his side.

"You!" he cried, recognising Caper. "You're behind this? That's not possible. How did you get through the Divide?"

"There's always a way," Caper replied.

"But why? Why are you following us?"

"You killed Knuth." Caper winced as the pain of the spines tickled the pain of the loss of his friend.

"Is that what this is about? You came after me because your leader was stupid enough to try that jump?" Wally could scarcely believe what he was hearing. "You tracked us all this way, you found a way to miraculously cross the Divide, you followed us across the river, and for what?

Revenge?"

"Of course."

A horrible thought suddenly twisted Wally's stomach. Had he unwittingly led this dingo all the way to this place just so he could play a part in the attack on Gus? Was it his fault that Gus was dead?

"So why attack Gus? Why not come after us?"

"The fox told me the three of you were in the den. He knew I'd go in after you, and he knew I'd be hit with those echidnas."

"He played you. Used you like a dumb mutt."

"Well, he's not so smart now, is he?"

Wally saw the spines in Caper's neck and chest, and the blood pooling in the dirt. At that moment he was gripped by an uncontrollable urge.

Wally approached the injured dingo without care. He stepped up to Caper and put his long foot across his neck, pinning his head to the ground.

He reached down to the spine that stood out from Caper's ribs and let his paws wrap around the quill. As his grip tightened, a surge of power raced through him, the power of life and death in his own small hands. He could end this now, with one swift thrust of the spine into Caper's heart. He *should* end this now. The dingo had followed him for weeks, through impossible barriers. Wally knew he would never give up.

"I'm so tired of running," he thought, as his fingers closed around the spine. Gus was dead because of this dingo. Wally felt his anger rise, felt it justifying his actions. The power was his now, the power of the predator. One sharp push and he could end the miserable beast, once and for all.

Wally braced himself to drive the spine home. Caper winced in fear, knowing what was coming.

One push is all it would take. Just one push.

Wally hesitated, suddenly seeing through his fury. "That's not what I am. Not who I am. I don't kill other animals for the sake of it."

"Hold still," he said, as he drew the first spine out of Caper's ribs.

"What are you doing?" asked Caper.

"What does it look like?"

"But I've tried to kill you. Why are you helping me?"

"Because you need help." Wally removed the second spine from Caper's neck.

Wally leaned in, putting his weight on Caper's neck and looked him straight in the eye.

"I'm leaving here, and you will not follow. I don't know how you got through the Divide, but there's plenty here for you. I will not see you again. Do you understand?"

Wally pushed off Caper's neck, and Caper raised his head to look at Wally with nothing but disgust in his eyes.

"If you think this changes anything between us, you're mistaken. You're weak. You could have finished this, but you just couldn't do it, could you. You can't change who I am. I'll get over this, and I'll be straight back on your trail. You keep looking over your shoulder, wallaby, because one day I'll be right there."

"You might. Or you might not. You're broken, dingo. You're not just hunting for food anymore. There's a sickness in you, and that sickness will take you long before you take me."

Wally turned and made his way back up the path, leaving the helpless dingo lying in the dirt.

THE DISTANCE

Jake found Wally on the ridge, staring off into the distance.

"It's a long way to go," he said.

"It's always a long way to go," Wally replied solemnly. "As if we haven't travelled far enough already."

"What's up with you?"

"I'm just tired of it," said Wally. "All of it. I really thought we'd arrived when we came through the Divide. I thought we'd finally made it. But it hasn't turned out anything like I imagined. I mean, we've got plenty to eat now and plenty to drink, but that mob! I knew there was something wrong there, but I didn't even think of the possibility of danger. We were joining a mob to get away from danger."

He paused for a moment before continuing. "I nearly got us all killed at the Divide, and I nearly got us all killed at Rocky Hill. I'm on a roll."

"Well, we're all still here, aren't we?"

"Then that miserable dingo shows up and plays a part in killing Gus. I can't help but think that was my fault."

"You can't be responsible for that, so stop beating yourself up about it. I don't know how that dingo got through the Divide, but there's no way you could've known about that, and there's nothing you can do about it now. Better to fight the battles in front of you, mate. You can't win the ones behind you."

"Well, there's plenty of time for that, then. Look at what's in front of us. This river winds its way to forever. That's how long we'll be travelling before we reach the end of it."

"Come on, mate. You never said it would be easy. Forget about what's ahead for a minute and look back at how far we've come. This has been the adventure of a lifetime, and really, would you take any of it back? We didn't leave our mob because things were going great. For all we know, our old mob might have starved to death by now. We were desperate. I still remember when you said, 'I have to leave'. I honestly didn't believe you'd do it. I nearly just rolled over and went back to sleep that morning. But I knew there was a chance, maybe just a tiny chance, that you would leave. And if you did, I didn't want to be left behind.

"There's no way I would have had the courage to head off on my own like you were going to. Remember that? On your own, Wally! Insane!" He laughed and gave Wally a good-natured shove.

"Anyway, I'm glad I showed up that day, and I wouldn't give a single jump back," Jake continued. "Not even if it meant getting the rest of my tail back. We've got plenty of food, plenty to drink, and this time we've got directions! I'd say things are looking up, wouldn't you?"

Wally looked over at Jake as the words sank in.

"I suppose," he said, starting to feel a little better. "What on earth would I have done without Jake and Peg?" he thought. The journey wouldn't have been the same without them.

"So, what do you think this ocean place is like?" Wally asked.

"Well, we'll never know if we keep standing here wondering."

Just then there was rustling in the bushes behind Jake and Wally. The pair swung around to see a large male wallaby from the Rocky Hill mob standing before them.

"You're not an easy bunch of wallabies to find," he said.

"We don't aim to be," replied Wally. "And now that you've found us, you can head straight back to your mongrel mob, because none of us are going back with you."

"I'm not here to take anyone back," the wallaby said, surprised by Wally's reply. "I came to ask if we could come with you."

"Who's 'we'?"

As if on cue, three more wallabies emerged from the thick bush, all female, one with a joey.

"Oh, perfect," said Wally.

"I know it's an imposition," the wallaby continued, "but we heard what happened to you at the rock pit. No one in that mob has ever had the guts to stand up to Doogan the way you three did. Most of the wallabies hate the mob. It's not even a proper mob, just a collection of leftovers from all the mobs that lived in the area before the dogs arrived. The rocks provide shelter for some, particularly the leaders, but the rest just sit and wait for their turn with the dogs. It's pathetic, really. So we decided to leave."

"And if we refuse?" asked Wally.

"We'll just do what you three have done, leave the mob and start our own little band. It seems to have worked out pretty well for the three of you."

Jake started to laugh a deep belly laugh, and the more he thought about what the wallaby had just said, the harder he laughed.

"There's no coming back. You know that, don't you? You'll be banished," said Wally, echoing words from what felt like a lifetime ago.

"Banished? That would be a good thing. We should've left a long time ago."

Wally saw a part of himself in the wallaby, in his resolve, his determination, and his spirit. He knew he could never find it in himself to refuse them.

"All right. You can join us. But it's a long journey ahead. We're going to the ocean. Apparently, it's at the end of the river."

"What's at the ocean?" the wallaby asked.

"The end of another adventure," Jake announced with a wide smile.

The wallaby turned to the others, who all nodded their approval.

"That's okay with us," he said.

"Just don't slow us down," Wally added wearily, just as Peg came bounding up the hill to join them.

"What's going on?" she asked, surprised at the sight of the four wallabies from the Rocky Hill mob and Jake still chuckling.

"These wallabies want to leave their mob. They've asked to join us," said Wally.

"Good move," said Peg, looking them over. "Well, you can't be all bad if you want out of that mob."

"I said it would be okay."

"Well then," said Peg, "we may not have found a mob, but it appears we may have just become one. That's seven, eight with the joey, and nine including Darcy. That sounds like a mob to me."

Wally turned to Peg. "Are we ready to go?"

"Yes," she replied. "Needles and Pins are still pretty upset, but I gathered some flowers with them, for Gus. They'll be okay."

She paused, then changed the subject to fill the silence.

"How's the knee?"

"Wobbly. As ever."

"Good," she said with a cheeky smile. "Well, come on then. I'll race you all down to the river."

And with that, she bounded down the hill, a sugar glider on board and seven wallabies in pursuit, leaving the Rocky Hill mob behind.

Epilogue

"Now that's what I call a wall," said Horatio. The two Tasmanian devils stood at the base of the Divide, the stony cliff towering above them.

"I've seen bigger," replied Bongo.

"Oh really? Bigger than that?" Horatio asked doubtfully. "Where?"

"You should spend a bit of time on the north side once in a while. Then you'll appreciate some real countryside. We've got walls twice the size of this."

"I think you'll find we've got countryside in the south too, thank you."

"You've got a couple of rivers and you think you've got it all. Try Cradle Mountain, that's countryside."

"Oh, it's just a mountain. Just like any other mountain."

"Shows how much you know," growled Bongo.

"So, what do we do now?" asked Horatio, sensing another fight brewing.

"Well, we're not going to get up those boulders, are we? Not unless you can sprout wings and fly us to the top. I'm going to try that ramp. Maybe that's how you get across."

The two devils made their way up the ramp, oblivious to all the strife that had occurred just a short while ago. As they reached the top and approached the edge, they looked down to see Caper's tree wedged against the rocks, forming a bridge from just under the Leap across to the ledge on the other side.

"Look at that. A bridge. I knew there must be a way," said Bongo.

Horatio looked at the narrow log that spanned the chasm. "It looks a bit dangerous, don't you think?"

"Dangerous? For heaven's sake! You are a Tasmanian devil. We live for danger! At least I do. 'Danger' is my middle name," he boasted, starting down the narrow path that led to the tree bridge. "Although, come to think of it, I don't actually have a last name."

Bongo made his way to the start of Caper's bridge. He climbed over the rocks and stepped onto the log without so much as a second thought, his mind clearly occupied with something far more important.

"But if I don't have a last name, 'Danger' can't

really be my middle name, can it?" he mused as he began to make his way across. "Maybe 'Danger' is my last name. 'Danger' or maybe 'Fearless' or 'Brave'. But then I'd need a middle name like 'the' if my last name was 'Brave'. Bongo the Brave! Yes, that sounds quite catchy," he said, pleased with himself.

"How about 'Bongo the Brainless'?" Horatio shouted as he watched Bongo make his way effortlessly across the narrow log, with only his balance separating him from a fall of certain death.

Bongo jumped off the trunk and onto the ledge on the other side. "Another victory for Bongo the Brave!" he declared. He turned to see Horatio still standing on the far side. "Are you coming or not?" he yelled impatiently across the chasm.

"Unbelievable," Horatio muttered, following Bongo's path down to the log. He placed two feet on it and looked down into the depth of the chasm. "Good heavens! It's a long way down!"

"You're not going that way," Bongo replied, as though it were the stupidest thing he had ever heard. "It's not that far along the log," he shouted, starting to lose his already precious patience.

Horatio stared deeper into the chasm and saw the bodies of the three dingoes. "There are dead animals down there! They must have fallen off the bridge!"

"Where?" asked Bongo doubtfully. "Oh, a couple of dead animals. Who cares about them? Actually, maybe we could have stopped for lunch. Oh well, too late for that now. Anyway, there aren't any Tasmanian devils down there, are there? They've all made it across."

"We are the only two devils here!" roared Horatio.

"Oh, come on. Either cross or don't cross, but I'm not coming back over there to get you. And don't worry, if you don't cross, I'll be sure to tell everyone back home what a courageous and savage beast you really are."

Horatio looked at the log, then down at the drop, then over at Bongo.

"If that idiot can do it, then so can I," he mumbled under his breath.

He stepped out onto the log. "Focus on the path. Focus on the path," he repeated to himself as he made his way slowly out over the abyss.

"You're not scared of falling, are you?" taunted Bongo. "You are! You're scared! Who can't walk across a log like that! Hey, Horatio! Don't look down, whatever you do!"

"Keep quiet!" Horatio shouted, the fear now turning his stomach into knots. Each step became a terrifying battle with vertigo. He was about halfway across when Bongo decided to have some fun.

"Oooo," he squealed in a high-pitched voice, "don't fall, Horatio, don't fall!" He put both feet on the log and started to bounce, sending tremors down the bridge.

"Stop it!" Horatio screamed, feeling the wobble under his feet. He quickened his pace, his anger now challenging his fear. He was three quarters of the way across when a loud crack rang out through the bush.

Time stopped for a moment as the log seemed to pause, deciding how it was going to split, before it started to give way. In moments of sheer desperation, true land speed records are often set, though rarely measured, but there was no question that, on that day, Horatio set the record for an unassisted Tasmanian devil, as he bolted down the collapsing bridge to the other side. He collected Bongo on his way through with such force that he drove him back from the ledge and into the cliff with a solid thud. Immediately, another violent altercation ensued as Caper's broken bridge crashed onto the rocks below.

"You lunatic! You could have killed me!" cried Horatio. "Have you lost your mind? Oh sorry, silly me, there was nothing to lose, was there?"

"What are you whinging about? You made it across, didn't you? If you hadn't spent half the day coming over, I wouldn't have had to encourage you."

"Encourage me? You are impossible!"

Furious, Horatio started up the trail that led to the lookout, with Bongo's mumbled protests trailing behind him. As he reached the lookout he stopped in his tracks, gazing down at the land below. Suddenly the fight was a distant memory as his eyes absorbed the view.

"Wow," he said, as Bongo came up to join him, and he fell silent too. The two devils just sat for a time, in silence, as they looked out over the lush, green land.

"Much better, don't you think?"

"Yes," replied Bongo quietly.

Horatio looked over at Bongo and saw tears in his eyes.

"What's wrong with you?"

"Nothing."

"Come on, give it up. What's the matter?"

"It reminds me of home," said Bongo softly. "It reminds me of home."

The End.

If you enjoyed this book, please consider writing a review on the site where you purchased the book. It may help spread the word about the state of the wallaby populations in Australia and raise awareness of the increasing and alarming rate of animal extinction on the planet.

Every voice counts.

For more information about the book, including the animals that feature in the book, please visit:

www.thewobblywallaby.com

THE PARMA WALLABY

In 1960 the Parma wallaby was considered extinct on mainland Australia. In 1965 an attempt was made to re-introduce the species back into Australia from a stock of Parma wallabies that had been captured and transported to Kawau Island, New Zealand, in the 1870s, by Sir George Grey, the then Governor of New Zealand but the re-introduction did not occur.

In 1967 a small number of Parma wallabies were discovered near Gosford in New South Wales (Australia) and further small populations of the species have been found in the northern parts of the state.

The Parma is the smallest of the macropods, is a solitary and mostly nocturnal animal and often sports a white moustache.

In addition to its native predators, mainly dingoes and eagles, the Parma suffers predation from many introduced species, including feral cats, wild dogs and foxes.

The Australian population of Parma wallabies remains under threat, the NSW Government currently lists the Parma as a near threatened species.

ACKNOWLEDGMENTS

Thank you again to Gabrielle Johnson for her ever-vigilant eye and of course, thanks again to Ruby for her enthusiasm and encouragement.

Also in this series...

The Wobbly Wallaby

A book about courage.

A mob of wallabies lies on the brink of starvation when a drought strikes the harsh Australian outback. Unwilling to endure the conditions any longer, a single wallaby with a bad knee gathers the courage to leave the protection of the mob to seek out a better place.

Joined by two of his closest friends, the trio begin a wild adventure through the perilous and unforgiving land. Danger follows in every footstep, until they are finally forced to confront their gravest fear...

The dingoes.

Also in this series...

The Way Home

The Wobbly Wallaby 3

"You have to see it for yourself, Wally, to understand how it connects everything. Just follow the river, it will take you there..."

Wally's journey through the Australian outback promises to deliver him to a place beyond his imagination, but only if he can overcome the greatest challenge of all...

Discover how Wally's epic journey ends in the third and final adventure in the Wobbly Wallaby trilogy.